# A Hard Day at the Holy Office

The Select Committee on Liturgical Vestments has been meeting daily for the past fifteen years in a forgotten corner of the Lateran Palace in Rome. But what connection is there between the activities of this bureaucratic relic and the world-wide ramifications of the Vatican intelligence net-work that has its secret headquarters in a complex of bunkers under St Peter's Square? And how did the Waynflete Professor of Statistical Historio-graphy come to be marooned in a lost monastery in Abyssinia? Why is Mrs Trigger suddenly seized by an uncontrollable desire to make love to a safe? What is the Negative-Sum Game? Who is Qu'at working for? What lies behind the door marked JANITOR?

Having read this novel, you may know all the answers. Or you may only think you know. For illusion and delusion on a huge scale are the theme of this Kafkaesque send-up of the Security Estab-lishment.

# A Hard Day at the Holy Office

## ROGER JONES

LONDON · W. H. ALLEN · 1970

© ROGER JONES, 1970

PRINTED IN GREAT BRITAIN BY
THE NORTHUMBERLAND PRESS LTD
GATESHEAD ON TYNE
FOR THE PUBLISHERS
W. H. ALLEN & CO. LTD
ESSEX STREET, LONDON WC 2

BOUND IN BUNGAY BY
RICHARD CLAY (THE CHAUCER PRESS) LTD

ISBN 0 491 00224 6

for
JOHNNY BYRNE
(without whom, etc.)

'Atención al informarse. Vívese lo más de información: es el oído la puerta segunda de la verdad, y principal de la mentira. La verdad ordinariamente se ve; extravagamente se oye; raras veces llega en su elemento puro, y menos cuando viene de lejos; siempre trae algo de mixta de los afectos por donde pasa. . . .'

GRACIÁN: *Oráculo manual*

THE STORY SO FAR:

Jubal Garforth FLAKE holds, or held, the chair of Statistical Historiography at the University of Oxford.

In a moment of moral unbalance the Professor permits himself an ill-judged attempt on the virtue of Miss Rowena THIRKELL. Miss Thirkell, unfortunately is as modest as she is desirable, and, even more unfortunately, her uncle is a Roman bishop of known piety. Most unfortunate of all, Miss Thirkell finds the Professor highly resistible. In the ensuing fuss Flake, having sown his wild oats (albeit on stony ground), reaps the whirlwind: his superiors, with a view to appeasing the bishop and at the same time banishing the fetid breath of scandal from the Senior Common Room, grant him a compulsory sabbatical leave of indefinite duration.

But already Dark Forces are at work, subtly reshaping the Professor's destiny. Unbeknownst to himself Flake's activities have caught the attention of Cardinal POLENTA, self-appointed watchdog of the Church's purity. For the moment the Cardinal's agents content themselves with bringing to bear on the unsuspecting academic a surveillance that is at once discreet, sinister and unrelenting.

Flake, unaware that his steps are marked, takes ship, more or less blithely, for the Continent. Even had he known that he had already earned himself a Red File in the Cardinal's archives, he might have supposed this to be simply another result of his tempestuous and futile amourette; he could not have known that the Cardinal's thought police are less interested in his morals than in the subversive heterodoxy of his teachings. He would certainly have found it hard to believe, had anyone told him, that the ultimate cause of his downfall was his *Statistical Aspects of the Diaspora with Special Reference to the Reign of Julian the Apostate*—the very paper that had won him his Chair.

Flake makes his way to Paris and puts up at an unclassified

hotel in the Place de la Contrescarpe. When this establishment is closed for reasons of 'moral hygiene' in a dawn raid by a flying column of hard-bitten specialists from the local prefecture, Polenta's men lose the Professor's trail.

Meanwhile Miss Thirkell, repenting her youthful folly, is desirous of quitting for ever the scene of her near-disgrace. She goes to London. There, on the recommendation of her uncle the Bishop, she is engaged in the role of secretary by Father MACCORD, manager-in-chief of a well-respected firm of ecclesiastical outfitters.

Polenta's agents pick up Flake's trail in Djibouti. But it is a cold trail—Flake has already departed for an unknown destination. Such information as they are able to obtain—scanty, garbled and of doubtful veracity—comes from interrogation of one PORSON or PERSON, a journalist of the worst sort and a third-degree alcoholic to boot. It appears that Porson, declared non grata in practically every state on the African continent (including Tchad, but excluding Basutoland and Upper Volta) has made his way to Djibouti. There, in a low grade maison de passe, he has made the acquaintance of the exiled Professor. Subsequently he seems to have succeeded in enlisting Flake's co-operation in some kind of nightmarish publicity stunt destined, apparently, to recoup their respective fortunes—both men being professionally and morally at the end of their tethers.

Beyond this point Porson's testimony is useless, Porson having relapsed into the screaming horrors to which he was intermittently prone. Whatever Porson's scheme was it must have been a miserable failure as far as publicity is concerned; Flake has disappeared without trace and Porson looks like being declared non grata in Djibouti.

Cardinal Polenta, however, is not particularly concerned about Flake as such. The Professor is no more than an infinitesimal part of the mighty jigsaw puzzle Polenta is assembling, piece by careful piece. Indifferent to the random behaviour of minutiae, he pursues his Grand Design.

NOW READ ON. . . .

*Part One*

# FLAKE

# I

The Select Committee on Liturgical Vestments met daily in a fourth-floor back room of one of the remoter wings of the Lateran Palace. Its mission was to enquire into possible changes in clerical outfitting with an eye to bringing traditional fashions more into line with current trends.

The decision to meet in the Lateran rather than within the confines of the Vatican City had lain with the Chairman of the Committee, Cardinal Polenta; and he had made his choice not from modesty but from caution. The Committee had been set up some fifteen years and three Popes earlier in a heady moment of modernising zeal, since passed. However, it chanced that the present incumbent of the Chair of St Peter was known to take a lively personal interest in the Vestment Situation—an interest which Cardinal Polenta found inconvenient if not downright dangerous and caused him to bless the foresight which had led him to place a substantial piece of the Eternal City between the habitat of His Holiness and his own stamping grounds.

It was with chagrin and alarm, therefore, that Polenta hurrying one morning to a meeting, found himself face to face, in a dusty corridor not fifty yards from the door of his Committee-Room, with H.H. in person.

'Ah! Cardinal Polenta!' exclaimed H.H. He didn't actually say 'Fancy meeting you *here*' but he tried, unsuccessfully, to convey the impression that he had not been loitering with intent in this particular corridor at this particular time, or, if he had been, it was with some other intent altogether.

Glowering inwardly Polenta bent to kiss the ring, which H.H. then wiped in a furtive and unconscious gesture on the seat of his white satin robe.

'And when can we expect your report, Polenta?' enquired H.H. as though the question had just occurred to him. 'You must know how eagerly we await its appearance.'

Polenta straightened, searching for a suitable reply. Finally he muttered, 'We're still hearing the evidence, Your Holiness.'

'Evidence?' H.H. was a little jarred by Polenta's choice of words.

'Evidence,' repeated Polenta, uncompromising.

'A long job, we imagine?'

'There is a great deal of evidence, Your Holiness,' said Polenta with a charged and piercing look. 'And one must be Thorough.'

'Of course, of course,' said H.H. hurriedly, a little dashed but trying not to show it. 'Well . . .'

He took off his little gold-rimmed spectacles and began to polish them with a cambric handkerchief he got from his sleeve. Polenta decided the interview was at an end and half turned to go. H.H. began to speak again.

'Er!'

Polenta stopped.

'Listen . . . I've got some . . .' H.H. dropped the plural pronoun and his voice to a whisper, '. . . designs . . .'

'Designs? Designs?'

'Oh, the merest sketches, daubs. The dabblings of an amateur. Hardly worth mentioning. A cope or two, some ideas for a new mitre. I don't like to trouble you . . . ?'

He broke off and eyed Polenta anxiously. Polenta looked back, gloomily. H.H. by now was wilting with embarrassment and his glasses were beginning to steam up again. Polenta decided to make a big effort (a policy decision).

'Not at all,' he said at last.

'Splendid,' cried H.H., beaming with pleasure and relief. 'I'll send them round then?'

'An honour, Your Holiness.' Polenta dragged his lips into what was meant for a gracious smile but looked more like an unforeseen side-effect of rigor mortis.

'Your opinion means a great deal to us, Cardinal Polenta,' said H.H. rubbing his hands, brisk again.

'Designs, yet!' moaned Polenta to himself as he went on his way.

'Something odd about that chap,' said H.H. to himself as he went on his.

Following this incident Polenta had deemed it prudent to set up a one-man sub-committee to produce an 'interim' report. This placebo had the desired effect, namely of keeping H.H. off his back for a while; but Polenta still had to fend off from time to time polite enquiries regarding the imminence (or otherwise) of a 'final' report. These served to convince him that time was short and lent a new urgency to his work.

H.H. was practically the only man in the Vatican City who remained unaware that Polenta's Committee had long ago abandoned any pretence of an enquiry into priestly wardrobes.

# 2

The Gorge of the Blue Nile is generally reckoned to be a notable feat of natural engineering. Some say that it makes the Grand Canyon look like a gravy river in a plate of mashed potatoes.

From Bardar Giyorgis at the southern end of Lake Tana in Abyssinia, the River Abbai, Little Abbai or Blue Nile is un-navigable for three hundred miles of its length until its confluence with the River Dadessa at Sirba near the Sudanese border. The Nile Gorge proper accounts for only a hundred and thirty miles of this three hundred; but, consisting as it does of an unending series of impassable cataracts hemmed in on both sides by unbroken and unscalable rock walls up to three and half thousand feet in height, it is hardly surprising that the Gorge should for so long have defied penetration and so remained one of the few sizable pieces of the earth's surface to remain almost totally unexplored.

However, it is neither to its grandeur nor its savagery that the Nile Gorge owes its place in our story, but to the presence in it, one fine day towards the end of the rainy season, of Professor J. G. Flake, late of the University of Oxford.

Flake owed his presence in the Gorge to the merest accident.

At no time since leaving Djibouti had he been able to lay claim to any real measure of control over the balloon in which he travelled. And though balloon navigation is notoriously subject to the vagaries of wind and weather, in Flake's case the situation was aggravated by his lamentable inability to devote his mind properly to the job in hand. The theoretical aspects of ballooning exercised on his brain an attraction so powerful as to render him impervious to the practical necessities of his situation. The long hours between cast-off and splash-down he filled with inspired calculation of vectors and tensors, wind-speed, convection currents, thermal pockets and ad hoc astrogation; and this not merely failed to avert, but was a prime cause of, the final ignominious catastrophe. (*)

He found himself up to his neck in a pool of scummy green water.

The pool was separated from the river by a substantial sand-bar. Half-submerged, the sad ruin of what had once been a gay and noble Montgolfier, kept him company at a short distance.

At this point Flake might easily have given himself up to regret and morbid thoughts. Instead he hastened to remind himself that he was in all probability the first white man ever to set foot in this particular pool. He had no idea where he was, but optimism was one of his characteristics.

He waded out. Behind him a crocodile, the first of a numerous flotilla, sank a speculative tooth into the envelope of the balloon.

Standing on the bank he shook himself like a dog. This tactic was only moderately successful as he was insufficiently hairy to get dry that way. He could hear the air escaping from the

* See Appendix, I. Page 173.

14

balloon as the crocodiles stepped up their attack. He permitted himself one brief moment of regret—if only they had been able to afford something better than hot air to fill the balloon— helium, hydrogen even—things might never have come to this pass. . . . He shook himself again and looked about him.

The bottom of the gorge at this point was about a mile wide. The river hugged the wall on the side furthest from him, moving fast in a roar of white water, penned against the far wall by a kind of moraine of sandbanks and tumbled rocks. He was standing on a level crescent of stony ground perhaps two miles in length, dotted with scrub grass and twisted thorn trees. The ends of the crescent were pinched off where the rock walls swung in to meet the river. On either hand the red cliffs jumped up and towered away in huge sweeps to meet the trailing edges of the sky.

The sun hammered the ground flat and the air above the canyon floor danced and reverberated, reeling in the heat.

Flake concluded his inspection, unwrinkled his eyes and lowered the hand which he had clamped explorer-fashion across his forehead. He removed his shirt as a prophylaxis against malaria. It is highly dangerous to let a wet shirt dry on your back in fever country. Unfortunately there was nothing he could do about the bilharzia he had doubtless contracted during his immersion in the pool.

When the silence became embarrassing, he coughed and said, 'Hum, a stroll is in order. If we are ever to get out of this place.'

He waited a little, coughed again and said, 'Down to the end then?' and set off.

In this way he came to the village.

It was nothing very splendid—a couple of dozen huts squatting irrelevantly at the base of the overhanging cliffs, almost hidden in a jumble of rocks.

The land around was cultivated and divided into plots by thorn hedges. Numbers of scrawny bullocks wandered about singly, or stood in groups moodily contemplating their exclusion from these little edens of melons and mealies. On their rumps most of the cattle bore evidence of having been subjected to the living-larder treatment.

The huts, crudely made of mud bricks, were cylindrical in shape, red-brown in colour, windowless, and fitted with low-pitched thatch roofs. Occupying a dominant central position was a much larger structure, also cylindrical, but painted white and surmounted by a cross; Flake supposed this to be a church, on the sound Occamist principle that if it wasn't, the cross was going to take a good bit of explaining.

There seemed to be no one about. A dog sat in a doorway biting itself. There were flies everywhere. Among the buildings nothing else moved. The principal evidence of human occupation was the sour, pervasive smell of burning dung.

The buildings were arranged, if that is the right word, higgledy-piggledy, in a way which suggested a heuristic rather than a rigidly formal approach to urban planning. There was nothing resembling a street. Flake zigzagged tiredly among the buildings, making for the church. From it came a sound of human voices raised in a communal droning.

'Sunday,' said the Professor with a hint of I-might-have-known-it.

He stopped in the entrance of the church. The rough wooden door stood open, but the building was windowless and the interior impenetrably black to eyes attuned to the midday glare outside. The liturgical wailing died raggedly to nothing. For a moment there was total silence.

'Anybody home?' he called.

Privately he judged this enquiry to be a triumph of controlled histrionics: it was delivered in a firm voice, but tinged with apology; pitched sufficiently low to convey respect for the precinct and a general readiness to conform within reason to the demands of local feeling and taboo; but at the same time sufficiently high to affirm the latent unwillingness of the sahib to be messed about by any undue prankishness on the part of the autochthons.

There was a further moment of silence. Then a crescendo of swishing, scraping and rustling as the congregation began to press towards the exit. Flake found himself forced gently but inexorably out of the doorway and back out into the sunshine.

They arranged themselves around him in a circle of two arm's length's radius, and waited. The Professor took stock. There were perhaps a hundred of them, hairy, bearded, barefoot and wearing floor-length black robes.

There were no women and no children.

The attitude of the crowd towards their visitor seemed to be compounded of mild surprise and polite curiosity; and though this was tinged in individual cases with more vigorous emotions —shock, incredulity, amusement—the general tone of the meeting was way short of hysterical. They simply stood around the Professor and watched him in silence.

Nothing happened for nearly five minutes. Everybody waited.

The Professor, always a high scorer in social perceptivity tests, saw that it was his move. He would have to say something.

He cleared his throat.

He was not among those who believe that to get through round or over the language barrier it is enough to speak loudly and carry a big umbrella. Besides, he had no umbrella.

On the other hand he did believe (wrongly) in the Universal Language of Gesture. Relying heavily on dim memories of manuals of Redskin sign talk, avidly perused in boyhood, he launched on a vivid and highly circumstantial account of his arrival in the gorge and the perils of the voyage hither. He then touched on some of the salient features of his present situation (balloonlessness, doubts as to whereabouts, etc.), before going on to deal at length with his pleasure at finding himself so unexpectedly in such agreeable and distinguished company. He concluded by assuring them that his earlier pique at seeing his dirigible devoured by caymans was quite dissipated in joyous anticipation of the fruitful intercourse he confidently looked forward to in the immediate future.

Most of this was lies. But audience response, though restrained, seemed to be favourable. There were smiles and the odd murmur of approbation. No one actually clapped, but on the other hand Flake saw none of the significant forehead-tapping he had seen

17

so much of in Djibouti. He felt sufficiently emboldened to venture an enquiry, reverting to acoustic signals for the purpose:

'Tiffin time?' he asked.

# 3

The Committee currently had five members, six if Polenta is included. With Polenta, their total weight was 349 kilogrammes (stripped) and their combined ages 362. Responsibilities were allotted as follows:

Cardinal MENSCHMEYER (Germany)—*Liaison.*
Cardinal FEGATO (Italy)—*Infiltration and Subversion.*
Cardinal CHINGADA Y VACA (Mexico)—*Plans.*
Cardinal BALAI-ROSE (France)—*Secretary to the Committee.*
Cardinal NUVOLETTO (Italy)—*Liturgical Vestments.*

Cardinal Nuvoletto, let it be said at once, was a dead letter. This charming and harmless old gentleman, a hangover from the first days of the Committee, had retained his place by virtue of his extreme senility and total deafness. This happy combination of qualities meant that he posed no kind of threat to Security. He commonly slept through the major part of the proceedings. He had, it is true, a tendency to snore. This annoyed some, notably Menschmeyer who had urged his removal. He was overruled by Polenta on the grounds that the amiable old derelict was a useful camouflage.

Menschmeyer's dislikes didn't stop short at poor Nuvoletto. There was bad blood, too, between him and Fegato. This proceeded from the following cause: while Menschmeyer was happily liaising with everything from the Boy Scout Movement to the Opus Dei, Fegato was up to his neck in what he called 'wide-spectrum' infiltration of everything from Moral Rearmament to the Tontons Macoute. So far so good. But when it came to comparing notes—a thing Menschmeyer and Fegato could only with difficulty be brought to do—it was found that the organisations most liaised-with by Menschmeyer were, broadly speaking, the ones most infiltrated and subverted by Fegato. Among the areas in which their spheres of influence overlapped in this way were: the S.I.D., the S.I.O.S., 'Joint', the B.N.D., the M.A.D., the O.V.N., 'La Mano', the P.I.D.E., the H.O.P., the Legion of Mary, the H.R.B., the H.I.A.G., 'Occident', the M.I.R., the F.L.N., 'Spinne' and 'Odessa'. (*) No compromise solution had so far been found, there being no area of reason held in common by Menschmeyer and his antagonist. Strangely, however, the situation was not displeasing to Polenta himself. It was, he thought, no bad policy to have a foot in both camps of every pie you had a finger in.

Meeting time: 0900 hours. The Cardinals sat round a long table. Polenta at one end on a kind of throne, Fegato and Balai-Rose on his left, Nuvoletto at the far end, Menschmeyer and Chingada on Polenta's right. Menschmeyer and Fegato were placed opposite each other, the better to exchange steely glares.

Meetings began with a short player calling for instant, and preferably total, liquidation of the Forces of Evil. If implemented it would have rendered Polenta and his entire organisation redundant overnight and left the Church Militant fencing with shadows.

'Reports,' said Polenta.

Without a word, enacting a much-practised drill, Balai-Rose got to his feet and passed round the table collecting the reports. He placed them in front of Polenta and sat down. They were typed on blue paper. There were four of them. Nuvoletto had not submitted a report and no one would have read it if he had. Perhaps Nuvoletto knew this in some corner of his dried-up pea of a mind. Anyhow, he was already dozing.

'Problems,' said Polenta, ignoring the reports.

'Nothing,' said Menschmeyer.

'Nothing,' said Chingada.

* See Appendix II. Page 174.

'Nothing,' said Balai-Rose.

'One,' said Fegato.

'Copy,' said Polenta.

Balai-Rose got up again. He took a sheaf of yellow papers from Fegato, placed it in front of Polenta and returned to his seat. As Fegato was sitting next to Polenta, the distance covered by the file was considerably less than that covered by Balai-Rose. Polenta was not interested in time-and-motion but in order-and-regularity.

'Summary,' said Polenta, eyeing the report distantly but making no move to read it.

Fegato outlined the nature of the problem with a terse objectivity and a restraint which were, considering his national heritage, remarkable. An Anomaly had been reported in Sector Four. It was nothing very serious, but required, in his opinion, prompt handling.

Polenta listened with the closest attention. Anomalies were meat and drink to him. When Fegato had finished, Polenta said: 'Action?'

Fegato shrugged. 'A contract?' he suggested.

'Objections?' asked Polenta.

'The man is a useful agent,' said Menschmeyer.

'Was,' countered Fegato, a nasty gleam in his eye. 'But is now dangerous. This kind of thing could spread.'

'Vote,' said Polenta sharply, before Menschmeyer could reply.

Fegato, Balai-Rose and Chingada raised their hands. Menschmeyer ground his teeth, silently.

'Overruled,' said Polenta to Menschmeyer. And to Fegato: 'Details to Operations before twelve hundred.'

A man was dead.

There was a pause during which Nuvoletto could be heard breathing heavily. His mouth hung open in a toothless smile.

'That is all,' said Polenta.

The meeting had lasted seven and a half minutes.

# 4

[The following is an extract from the so-called *Abyssinian Journal* of Prof. J. G. Flake, edited by Cranley Heavenspur and published in *Proceedings of the Society of Statistical Historiographers* (Vol. XXXVI No. ix).]

The Monastery of the Blessed Shn'ut is located in a remote, and inaccessible section of the Nile Gorge at approximately 36°12′E 10°34′N. . . . Of the Blessed Shn'ut himself, founder of the community which bears his name, we know little with any degree of certainty. The saint's name is normally qualified by the sobriquet 'Shenouda' which may (Or may not—Ed.) be a corruption of the Amharic 'shnadu', meaning 'needy' or possibly 'keen', 'eager'. Alternatively this appellation may originally have been applied to distinguish him from his better-known near-namesake Shenute, Shnuti or Schnudi (333–?450) founder of numerous desert monasteries in Skete and the Thebaid. (See 'La Vie de Schnoudi' tr. Amerlineau, and my Note below. Ed.)

Shn'ut, we are told, came originally 'from the North' (?Upper Egypt) and settled in the highlands of central Abyssinia, probably in the region of Debra Tabor. No date can be assigned to this event but we may safely assume it to have been associated with the conversion of Abyssinia to Monophysite Christianity under the Patriarch of Alexandria in the fourth century of our era.

Here Shn'ut devoted himself to preaching and conversion, both by word and example. Levitation, troops of devils put to flight, extraordinary austerities, raising the dead (sometimes on quite trivial pretexts), friendship with lions—these and other manifestations of exceptional sanctity were everyday matters to Shn'ut. He soon attracted a numerous following. As his fame spread, a large and flourishing monastic community sprang up around him, dedicated to the 'Rule of the Short Stick of the Blessed Shn'ut'. Precise details of this rule are lacking. It is clear, however, that the 'Stick' played a crucial part in spiritual exercises of the saint's followers, both men and women. In the light of what is known of the severe, almost sadistic, discipline of the Egyptian communities of the period, it is possible that the phrase 'short stick' designates some instrument of punishment, probably of flagellation. On the other hand, most references to its use imply that the ritual of the Stick was a pleasurable, even an ecstatic experience. And it is curious that it appears to have been popular with the saint's numerous women disciples, who are specifically stated to have been 'particularly zealous' in the practice of the Rule.

All went well for many years. Under the eye of the Saint and the guidance of the Prophet Isaiah, Shn'ut's personal patron, the flock of the faithful grew steadily in numbers, enthusiasm and spiritual excellence. However, when the Blessed Shn'ut was declining in years and 'exhausted by his labours' a dispute arose which was to have a tragic outcome. The issue, evidently, concerned the Founder's continued fitness for his task. Dissatisfaction led to protest, protest to contention. Shn'ut insisted that he was willing to continue but the Prophet (Isaiah) would not have it. The argument grew more bitter. The community split down the middle. For reasons which are obscure the male members of the group took Shn'ut's side against the women. Feelings ran high, blows were exchanged, blood spilled, and before long a state of open war prevailed. The conflict, animated as it was by a combination of religious and sexual antipathies, was unrestrained, brutish and bitter. The men, being the less numerous, had the worst of it. Finally Shn'ut himself was forced to fly for his life, taking with him the few of his followers who had survived, 'all old men'. They 'took the way south, to the river' where, shaken and dispirited, they were brought to a stand by their sudden arrival on the clifftops of the Nile Gorge. Their strength at an end, a long drop in front of them, the halloos of their pursuers in the woods behind—nothing short of a top-flight miracle could save the Saint and his party from the fate of King Pentheus.

At this desperate juncture the prophet Isaiah materialised and 'greeting them in a friendly way laid hold of the Short Stick of the Holy Man, under which influence the Stick extended itself until it reached the bottom of the chasm. Down the ladder so formed the followers of the Saint descended one by one until in this way they arrived below, safe and whole. But the Blessed Shn'ut remained alone above them on the cliff's edge. Then the Prophet took the Saint in his arms and bore him safely and tenderly through the air and brought him again to his companions waiting below. They congratulated each other and thanked God for their deliverance.'

Having no option, the group decided to settle in the Gorge. They built a church at the precise spot where the feet of the Saint had touched-down, and dedicated it to the 'Miraculous Extension of the Short Stick'.

Shn'ut himself died soon after at the age of a hundred and thirteen.... (*Here there follows a long digression on the significance of this number*—Ed.) He was buried in the church which became his shrine. In its present form it contains relics of the Saint and is decorated with murals depicting incidents in his life. There is a particularly fine 'Dormition' measuring thirteen and a half feet by seventeen above the central altar. . . .

*Editor's note*: Professor Dobson, to whom I showed these pages, has suggested that a hitherto obscure passage in Evagrius Scholasticus, previously supposed to refer to Shenute the Egyptian, might in fact be a reference to Shn'ut the Needy. The passage in question is known to be slightly corrupt (see Krappner p. 280 et ff, Hausherr p. xvii) and the difference in the names may safely be attributed to a scribal error in transliteration.

The possibility is particularly fascinating for, if Professor Dobson's supposition is correct, this passage constitutes the only extant references to the Blessed Shn'ut in Western (i.e. non-Coptic) sources.

'There came to them out of the desert one (?Shn'ut) who had spent many years alone in the practice of virtue. Through which his soul and body had been raised so far above the influence of earthly passions that he returned to the town and mixed again with men. And the better to show that he was dead to the world, he feigned both madness and debauchery. He had no need of the good opinion of mankind, for he had long cast off vanity, which, as Plato tells us, is commonly the garment men are last to shed. He would appear to have dealings even with courtesans, staying for long periods shut up with them, and when he left their rooms, would come running out and throwing furtive looks all about him, the better to increase suspicion. As long as he remained there, before returning to the desert, he made a point of behaving always as if he had taken leave of his senses . . .'

*Ecclesiastical History (Lib. II cap. xiv.)*

# 5

There was a place by the river where a clump of stunted cotton-willows gave a little shade. Flake spent a lot of time here. He would sit for hours watching the river smash itself into a white mess against the granite reefs which barred its path, then on and away, sliding smooth again like some glossy black animal round a bend in the canyon and out of sight.

Often, during the hottest part of the day when the monks came in from the fields to rest and pray in their huts, Rasselas would join him under the trees and they would sit together, talking, or tending the fish trap they had built in a backwater nearby and which never caught anything but pebbles rolled by the current along the river bed.

On Flake's first arrival in the Gorge they had given him a hut to live in, and Rasselas, it seemed, was included in the lease as cook, interpreter and guide. Through him Flake had gone far towards mastering Amharic, the lingua franca of the community and meanwhile had developed a real affection for the little monk with his one good eye and his permanent grin entirely surrounded by beard.

One day Rasselas, after sitting for a long time in unaccustomed silence, turned to his friend and asked: 'Tiffin-time, how long have you been with us?'

Looking round Flake saw that for once the face he knew so well was completely serious. It looked wrong without its smile.

Flake thought for a moment.

'Ten months and twenty-one days.'

'Is it a long time?'

'Yes.'

Suddenly a picture came into Flake's mind of himself in a punt on the Cherwell . . . Yes it was a long time. When had he last had a cigarette?

'Tiffin-time, when you first came to us you asked many questions. You wanted to know many things.'

'Yes,' said Flake.

'And I answered your questions as well as I could.'

'Yes.'

'But some of your questions I could not answer, although I knew what was in your heart.'

'You knew?'

'I knew that you wanted to leave us.'

'You said there was no way.'

'There was no way.'

'But you came here, and the others. There is a way in. There must be a way out.'

'I have told you—'

'You told me that it was a miracle.'

'A *great* miracle,' Rasselas corrected him. For a moment the smile returned to his face, but it was a sad smile. He shook his head slowly several times from side to side.

'Tiffin-time, do you still wish to leave us?'

'Yes,' said Flake. He had the answer now: ten months, twenty-three days, seven hours. Or seventy-two thousand five hundred and fifty-nine hours. Allowing an average of one cigarette per hour he had saved six hundred and six pounds, four shillings at English prices.

Rasselas squinted at the sky, then stood up, brushing the dust from his black robe.

'Come with me now, Tiffin-time,' he said. 'I have something to show you.'

He led the way back to the village, walking slowly as it was very hot. There was no one about. It was the dead time. When they got to the Church, Rasselas stood back to let the Professor enter first. It was cooler inside. Flake could see nothing, but he felt the little monk's hand on his arm, guiding him forward across the floor. They stopped at the iconstasis which screened the altars from the main body of the church.

Soon his eyes had adjusted sufficiently to be able to pick out details in the yellow glow of the lamps which lit the window-less interior. His nose picked up the smell of incense—bark pounded with cow dung—and the musty smell which came from the packed-earth floor.

He heard Rasselas's voice, speaking softly beside him in the gloom: 'Go through. Look on the central altar and tell me what you see there.'

As he ducked through to the other side of the screen, Rasselas's anxious whisper came after him. 'Do not be long. You must not be seen here.'

Inside, Flake peered uncertainly about him at the unfamiliar surroundings. The sanctuary was a small space almost filled by its three altars and by a clutter of icons, statues, crosses, lamps, censers, and embroidered banners mounted in what looked like umbrella stands. Niches in the walls and in the screen held devo-tional lamps burning imperfectly purified animal fat. Rush dips flared smokily in the heavy air before the holy pictures on the two side altars. On the central altar stood a large cross and two large candles. And something else.

Flake went nearer and bent to look, craning his thin neck.

It was a box about fourteen inches long by eight square, made of thick glass panels set in a frame of some yellowish metal, brass perhaps, or gold. Peering close, and moving his head this way and that so as not to cut off the light, Flake was dimly able to make out what lay inside. It was a roughly cylindrical object, brownish in colour, its surface pitted, wrinkled and pocked to give it a texture like that of perished rubber, stretched

tight. He thought briefly of a section of hockey-stick handle—
some memory of his schooldays. Then another idea occurred to
him—a scroll, a manuscript. A distant tingle of scholarly excitement stirred in a corner of his mind.

Then he heard Rasselas cough nervously twice on the other
side of the screen. He straightened.

Rasselas's whisper: 'Come now, Tiffin-time. We must leave
this place.'

With a last puzzled look over his shoulder at the reliquary,
Flake passed through the screen. Rasselas was waiting for him
at the door, fidgeting.

The monk led him back to the river at a fast walk without a
word spoken. The sun was noticeably lower in the sky. Soon it
would drop behind the western wall of the canyon.

When they were seated again side by side on a rock over-
looking the water, Rasselas turned to his friend and, still in the
same serious manner, asked: 'You saw it?'

'I saw it.'

'And you felt the . . . ?'

He used a word of whose meaning Flake was uncertain.
Something like 'spirit' perhaps, or 'power'.

'I felt nothing.'

Rasselas seemed to relax a little. His shoulders slumped frac-
tionally in a movement of relief. Or was it disappointment?

'I did not think you would. I have not felt it myself. They
say it is only . . . women . . . who feel it.'

'Feel it? Feel what? I understand nothing in all this.' There
was an edge of irritation in Flake's voice.

Rasselas looked long and hard at him. There were tears in
the corner of his eye. 'My poor friend, I have shown you this
thing because I think you will leave us soon. Very soon. And I
wanted you to see it before you go.'

'Go? How? I understand nothing, I tell you. I have seen
what you wanted me to see. But I do not know what it was.
And you speak of my going, but—'

Rasselas raised a hand to cut him short.

'As for your going, I have already told you, it is . . .' he smiled '. . . a miracle. Soon you will see it and then you will have no more questions.'

'I still don't—'

'And as for what you have just seen—you cannot guess?'

'No.'

Rasselas turned his head away and looked fixedly down at the water. 'What you have seen today,' he said, 'is the whole reason for our being in this place. It is the Short Stick of the Blessed Shn'ut.'

# 6

The real nerve centre of Polenta's organisation lay neither in the Lateran Palace nor (strictly speaking) within the confines of the Vatican City, but in a complex of bunkers under St Peter's Square. These had been constructed during World War Two as a bomb-proof repository for certain of the Vatican treasures. Polenta had quietly made them his own in 1947 after a brisk contest for squatter's rights with a small army of Norway rats. Here Polenta proceeded to set up his GHQ—Situations Room, Communications Centre, Briefing and De-Briefing Halls, and a small chapel for the use of personnel not on duty.

And here, behind a fourteen-inch steel door marked 'Janitor', the Files were kept.

Polenta's collection of confidential dossiers—huge, meticulous, purposeful, unimaginably comprehensive, and Secret in the extreme—was a system built very much in his own image. Its foundations were, firstly, a passionate conviction that nobody, but nobody, is above suspicion, and, secondly, a collector's itch verging on the pathological.

He kept a file on everybody who was anybody and on as many people again who were no one at all. (Professor Flake, for example.) And, as such vast quantities of information necessitated an equal number of informants, all of whom had access, ex-officio, to confidential information and were therefore, by definition, Suspect, he kept files on his informants too. This made the whole thing self-perpetuating, like a yeast colony out of control.

The exponential growth rate of the collection had received a gratifying boost in the late 1960's. After one of the seismic security scandals which periodically rock the Italian defence establishment, Polenta, led by his collector's nose, had followed a minor ripple to an auction of 'surplus' dossiers organised by an enterprising functionary at the Ministry of Defence. The dossiers turned out to be top-classification SIFAR files, officially condemned but, as the official in question blandly put it, 'too good to burn'. There were nearly three thousand of them. Fortunately the Ministry man was a true son of the Church and proved amenable to reason. After a suitable number of reasons had changed hands the idea of an auction was quietly dropped, an equivalent number of genuinely valueless files was borrowed from the Ministry of Roads and Bridges and duly burned while Polenta, rejoicing, brought home the bacon. He was so elated by his acquisition that he classified the whole lot Red Ten out of hand without opening one of them. There were three colour-categories:

> WHITE (above suspicion)
> GREEN (bears watching)
> RED (suspect)

Category Red, being by far the largest, was further subdivided according to the *amount* of suspicion adhering to the subject. This quality was represented by a numerical scale running from 1 to 10 and known as the Unreliability Index.

Benefit of the doubt played no part whatever in the assigning of Unreliability Indices.

It is open to speculation whether these colours had any liturgical significance. Green, for instance, is traditionally the colour of Hope; and it is true that in former days the Cardinal had—rather naïvely perhaps—classed most of his own agents under this colour. But disillusionment and riper years had led to a succession of purges and pogroms accompanied by a massive Doppler shift towards the lower end of the spectrum. Now only a sad handful of Greens remained to testify to Polenta's youthful ingenuousness. Even these he privately thought of as potential Reds rather than potential Whites.

There were no files in the White category since the Cardinal had given up keeping a file on himself.

For light reading Polenta had Sarpi's 'Council of Trent' and Llorente's 'The Inquisition in Spain'. These he kept by his bedside and never opened. He had no time for light reading.

The file room itself had studiously been made proof against the most recherché disasters, ranging from Acts of God to mere larceny by teams of trained saboteurs armed with thermite rods, nitroglycerine and hydrofluoric acid. The door was endowed with a system of locks, alarms and booby-traps so complex and so time-consuming that the Cardinal was incapable of carrying in his head more than half the information required to get through it unscathed. Unwilling, on grounds of Security, to commit anything to paper, he memorised as many as he could of the necessary shibboleths and entrusted the remainder to Father Singleton, his Right Hand. 'Entrusted' may be too strong a word. What he had done was to teach Singleton a kind of catechism in which lay concealed all the necessary information —a tiny bit scrambled for safety's sake, but still viable. He had not thought it wise to let Singleton know the meaning of this little dialogue. Such knowledge would have rendered Singleton liable to a Red file and seriously diminished his utility. All that was needed was for Singleton to cough up the facts when called on to do so. The desired responses were elicited by a simple series of numerical triggers designed to minimise the amount of brainwork falling on the Cardinal himself.

A sample:

CARDINAL : Good morning, Singleton.
SINGLETON : (*respectful*) Good morning, Your Eminence.
(*Pause*)
CARDINAL : (*casually*) One.

SINGLETON: Right hand knob, Your Eminence.
CARDINAL: Well done, Singleton. Very good.
(*Pause*)
CARDINAL: Ah . . . Two?
SINGLETON: Revelations thirteen seven.
CARDINAL: Splendid, splendid. . . . THREE!
SINGLETON: Set oven to Regulo mark four, Your Eminence.

*Etc.*

As a device for limiting the load on Polenta's mnemonic powers, the system worked well. There was, of course, the risk that some accident—death, defection, or sudden and massive cerebral deterioration—might rob him of Singleton's services. But no contingency plan suggested itself that did not pose added problems, mainly in the field of Security. He might, for example, have got Singleton to enlist and train an understudy. But this would constitute a proliferation of sensitive information—a thing inherently repugnant to the Cardinal's nature. So he contented himself with frequently urging Singleton to 'take care of himself'. At the same time he gave instructions for a regular quota of prayers for Singleton's health to be addressed to the proper quarters. The text of these prayers, as laid down in Operational Instruction No. 247691, amounted in effect to an all-risks insurance cover. Special emphasis was laid on averting 'amnesia, aphasia, anomia, schizoid alienation, catatonic states of all kinds' and 'possession'.

These dispositions made, Polenta was still faced with the problem of how to open the door to the file room without Singleton, whose presence was a sine qua non, being aware of what was afoot. He had got round this by means of a set of remote controls in a drawer of his desk. This installation had been carried out at dead of night by technicians of the highest possible security ratings, and, on completion, important work had been found for them in leper colonies and Amazonian mission stations. Now all the Cardinal had to do was to appear to rummage idly in his desk drawer while putting Singleton through his paces, dismiss Singleton, cross to the door marked 'Janitor' (conveniently sited at one end of his office) and, secure from interruption, finish the process at his leisure.

Recently he had been spending more and more time in the file room, working on the List.

The List was the central fact of Polenta's life, the Secret of Secrets, Weapon of Weapons, the hammer he was forging to smash for ever the enemies of God.

Without the files, compilation of the List would have been impossible. Even with them it was a gigantic undertaking for one man working in secret and alone. When completed it would contain the name of every known or suspected heretic, crypto-schismatic and doctrinal deviant currently lurking in the broad bosom of Mother Church.

Heresies were arranged alphabetically: A for Arians, B for Bogomils, C for Cathars, D for Donatists (and Docetists), and so on. He had just completed M (Manichaeans) and was putting the last names under N (Nestorians). O'Toolites were next, and then Pelagians.

But time was getting short. The forthcoming Vatican Council was only months away.

The Council was Polenta's deadline.


# 7

Behind the village was the place Flake called the Crack. It was a deep cleft in the rock wall which angled back and away from the houses, forming a narrow, wedge-shaped canyon some seven or eight hundred feet from end to end, suggestive of a very thin slice of a very large cake. The sides were vertical, but the floor was choked with fallen rock—cake-crumbs—which formed a kind of scree sloping steeply up from the open end, so that the level of the innermost part of the fissure was approximately half-way between the floor of the valley and the top of the cliffs.

In the early days, searching for an exit from the valley, Flake had come several times to this place, but found it to be a dead end. The hundreds of feet of smooth rock-face which still stood between him and the outside world rose up around him as sheer and unclimbable here as at any other point. And because it was a depressing place, dark and narrow, and because he felt there like an ant that has ventured between the thighs of an elephant, he soon ceased to visit the Crack.

The day after Rasselas had taken Flake into the Church, the entire community assembled in the Crack. They had made their way up from the village at first light, in solemn procession with banners, icons and chanting, led by the Abbot under a large black umbrella, and now they stood jammed shoulder to shoulder in the highest and narrowest part of the fissure, still chanting, all eyes turned upward to the knife-edge of sky above their heads.

In the centre of the crowd one tiny space remained clear where a table or rock about six feet square formed a kind of natural dais.

Flake, hovering excitedly on the edge of the event, looked up like everyone else and waited. He had set aside his rational nature—a pardonable lapse in the heat of the moment—and was waiting anxiously for his First Real Miracle.

The waiting was prolonged until the sun shone directly into the Crack like a burning eye into some unimaginable plughole and the roof of sky blurred into a white ache where nothing could be seen.

Out of this blur came the Miracle. It consisted of a basket on the end of a long rope, lowered from above.

The chanting faltered for a moment, giving place to a gasp of communal fulfilment. Then it was taken up again, more vigorously than before, while the basket continued its descent until it all but touched the centre of the stone table. At this point two agile young monks, the skirts of their robes tucked into their belts, leapt on to the dais and gave a mighty jerk on the rope to signal a halt to the unseen mechanics above. The basket hung, spinning slowly, its bottom inches above the stone.

It was shaped like an elongated and deftly decapitated boiled egg. It measured about five feet in height by two feet across the middle. It was full of flowers. The two monks on the platform emptied these out, tossing them into the crowd. They were appreciatively received. Some of the monks put blossoms behind their ears. When the basket was empty, the workers round the basket began rapidly to fill it with small rocks, passed up to them by those standing nearest. This they continued to do until the basket was, in Flake's estimation, half full. Then another signal was given and the freighted receptacle rose jerkily but quickly into the air. Every eye followed it on its upward journey.

And lo! When it was half-way up, it was met by another basket coming down.

The new basket proved on arrival to contain a live human being. Half his frightened face came into view as he made his first survey of the world for which he had left the world for ever. The lift-men helped him to scramble out. He was no more than fifteen-years-old, barefoot, dressed in cotton drawers and shirt with a *chamma* over his shoulder. Two monks took him to the Abbot who embraced him and blessed him while the chanting swelled momentarily in pitch. Then, without more ceremony —they were anxious, perhaps, to forestall any last minute change of heart—the new recruit was led away through the crowd by his two escorts and down the rocky path towards the village.

Before the party had turned the first bend in the road, the basket had been refilled with stones and, to redoubled chanting, was rising again into the air.

Rasselas came burrowing through the crowd until he stood at Flake's elbow.

'I spoke to him,' he said excitedly. 'Eleven more are coming.'

'Twelve in all?' asked Flake.

'There was a time,' said Rasselas, 'when they came by twenties and by fifties. Once it took three days to bring them all down.'

Suddenly there was melancholy in his face.

'Counterweight,' thought Flake, in English.

34

'Now you see how it is done,' said Rasselas. 'Our miracle.'

Flake didn't answer, Rasselas looked at him sharply, suddenly realising that his friend's thoughts were elsewhere, realising too, with a quick pang, that Flake was already lost to him. And he knew that it had to be so and there was nothing he could do.

The second basket was already down with its load.

Rasselas put out a hand to take the Professor's arm and his fingers closed briefly in a gentle pressure. He took a long slow look at Flake's face. Then he removed his hand and was gone into the thick of the crowd. Flake didn't even notice him go. He began to edge forward unobtrusively towards the loading platform.

# 8

'How big?' asked the Editor, contemplating with some distaste the seedy, florid and malodorous figure sprawled in his second best chair.

'Big,' said Porson, 'huge.'

'Like the balloon thing,' sneered the Editor. 'That was big. Biggest fiasco ever to—'

'How the hell was I to know he couldn't fly the thing?'

'YOU COULD HAVE ASKED HIM,' yelled the Editor, nearly losing his grip. These freelance bastards were all the same, he thought. Liars and bunglers. 'You freelance bastards are all the same,' he said. 'Liars. Bunglers.'

A defiant gleam came into Porson's eye, such a gleam as might illumine the orbit of angler disbelieved in a truly gigantic lie.

'This is big,' he repeated stubbornly. 'Bigger than . . .' he searched for a metaphor.

The Editor eyed him acidly, fixed in a pose of patient exasperation. Cogs ground rustily in the wreckage of Porson's mind.

'Bigger than. . . . THE DEAD SEA SCROLLS!' he cried at last.

'It'd better be,' said the Editor.

There was a longish pause.

'All right, I'll buy it.'

Porson sprang to his feet with such a suddenness that the world slid away under him and he had to grab at the desk for support.

'When do I leave?'

'Yesterday . . . Now listen, scab. I don't trust you, and I wouldn't send you if there was anyone else who knew the area. If you fumble, it'll be the last fumble you ever do, for this paper or any other. Now get out.'

Porson had covered half the distance between himself and a large scotch before the Editor had his mouth shut.

That evening's edition carried the front page headline—

MISSING BALLOONIST BACK FROM DEAD.

And underneath, in print only slightly smaller—

'NEWS' EXPEDITION RESCUE BID DASH.

But Porson had no intention of doing any dashing until thoroughly fortified against the rigours of the trip. Towards closing-time he was slumped half across a table in the smoke-room of the Bird In Hand on the corner of Fetter Lane.

'Bigger than the Dead Sea Scrolls,' he muttered into the ash tray.

He had been saying the same thing all the evening. The colleagues who had clustered round and bought him drinks in the hope of a fast column or two without the trouble of leaving the pub had drifted disgustedly away to drink elsewhere. The only one left was 'Pappy' Simpson of the 'Echo' who was unable to drift anywhere, being too drunk to move. Simpson had been a crossword-setter for a time in his youth and thirty years later had still not managed to empty his head of the useless scraps of knowledge with which he had inadvertently stuffed it.

'Bigger than the Dead Sea Scrolls,' said Porson again.

Simpson leaned forward very slowly and peered into the ash-tray under Porson's nose as if to verify Porson's observations. Finally he said, very slowly and very seriously: 'There is only one thing which would be bigger than . . . that and that is . . . the Q text of the . . . gospels. *That* would be big if you like.'

Half a minute later Porson heard what Simpson had said. Something went clack inside his head. Porson had a mind like a steel trap, very little got in or out. It was, besides, a small mind and had room for only one idea at a time.

He looked up and peered soddenly across the table.

'Q text?'

'Q text,' Simpson affirmed, nodding six or seven times in slow motion. 'If you found *that*, what a story *that* would be.'

Porson digested this. Then a look of alarm invaded his face. 'SSHHHH,' he hissed.

# 9

Flake wasn't at all sure how he had got to Famaka after leaving the Gorge.

On the second day of the journey he had fallen in with a group of rather seedy Galla tribesmen. They were on their way to the plains to 'trade', as they gave him to understand, for cattle. Flake entertained private reservations about the business ethics of a group of merchants whose only luggage was a frightening variety of spears, clubs, pangas and rusty Italian rifles. Rather than wait for a fuller insight into local economic practices he had taken an early opportunity of striking out unobtrusively on his own. The parting was accomplished at night and without the formality of a goodbye. It was hastened by the Professor's growing conviction—born of a gleam at once speculative and possessive in their eyes whenever they looked at him—that they saw in him not so much a valued travelling companion as a capital asset on the hoof.

The remainder of the journey, recollected now only in patches, was invested in retrospect with the quality of an extended nightmare. It had ended with the Professor's arrival, tatty and half delirious, on the doorstep—or, more precisely, veranda—of one Nikos Kolofouskomenos, merchant, of Famaka. It was hazard that brought him there (his eyes had been shut at the time), but hazard could not have chosen a better doorstep to deposit him; for Mr Kolofouskomenos, known to Famaka's select European colony as Fat-ass Niko, combined the functions of proprietor of the Pantopoleion Athenaikon with those of British Consul.

The latter post he owed to the triumphant success of certain negotiations which had taken place between himself and H.M. Government some years previously. These negotiations involved, on the one hand, a stupendous quantity of rancid groundnut oil 'surplus to requirements', and on the other, exclusive development rights to rich and hitherto unexploited bauxite deposits ostensibly located 'in the Soddo-Gocho-Yambo area' (8°N 36°E). Whether H.M.G. actually believed either in the existence of these deposits or in Fat-ass Niko's right to dispose of them will never be known. For immediately after conclusion of the deal, reports of a particularly virulent outbreak of tularaemia in the target area were circulated and caused a sudden loss of interest in plans to exploit the concession. Any regrets H.M.G. might have felt at this turn of events were amply compensated by the ease with which so embarrassingly large a quantity of peanut extract had been cleared from its books. Fat-ass Niko, for his part, had little difficulty in finding local outlets for the oil, of whose value both as cosmetic and comestible he was fully aware. It was not long before rancid groundnut oil had established itself as the recognised medium of exchange from Gallabat to Gambela Post, replacing, while supplies lasted, all other currencies such as salt bars and brass cartridge cases. Mr Kolofouskomenos looked back on this incident as one of the most gratifying in a life dedicated to the practice of the 'combina' in all its forms.

It was seldom, though, that he was called on to fulfil the

functions of the office which had fallen to him among the fruits of his acumen. The post of British Consul in Famaka was little more than an unpaid sinecure. It carried status of course, but status butters precious few parsnips.

It was with lively emotion, therefore, that Fat-ass Niko had viewed the arrival of his very first, half-dead but wholly genuine, Distressed British Subject. He rose to the occasion. A message outlining the facts of the situation was drafted, addressed to the consulate at Khartoum, and despatched by messenger to Roseires where there was a telegraph station. It was not Niko's fault that the donkey-borne emissary was detained en route by the wedding of a distant cousin in an even more distant village —an irksome obligation which entailed a delay of five days, three for the feasting and two to get over it.

Meanwhile Flake was nursed back to health on a diet of beans and macaroni by Mrs Kolofouskomenou, and Fat-ass Niko taught him to play tavli. This kept them busy until the arrival of the helicopter bearing on one side the legend—

DAILY NEWS EAST AFRICAN RESCUE EXPDN

and on the other side—

HERZ RENT-A-CHOPPER

and on the inside, Porson.

The reception committee consisted of Flake, Fat-Ass Niko in a clean shirt, and the entire population of Famaka—some firing rifles into the air, others brandishing stocks of souvenirs for the attention of the visitors.

The helicopter was painted orange, very gay, and lettered in black.

From it emerged: first, a photographer; second, after a decent pause, Porson.

The photographer was hung about with some half dozen cameras of various calibres and capabilities, which he handled in a way which suggested that they were the weapons of a professional gunslinger. He began to exercise his profession as soon

39

as his feet touched the ground and ignored all attempts to shake his hand, sell him postcards, or interest him in services which ranged from straightforward portering to free introductions to relatives of all sexes.

The appearance of Porson was greeted by an increase in the tempo of applause and musketry. A group of local cargo-cultists ran forward and began to decorate the helicopter with flowers and garlands. One or two were felled by the still slowly turning rotors but the remainder persisted.

Porson, ex-machina, was anything but godlike—swaying, unshaven, his cotton suit stained and bagged, his tie askew, hair wild, eyes screwed up in an expression of bewildered agony, one hand clutching his headache and the other a bottle of Johnnie Walker, three parts empty.

He took several paces forward, staggering wildly with each step. The onlookers attributed his unsteadiness to a pardonable emotion. At this point he found himself confronted by Flake, who had his hand out in greeting. It was a charged moment. A temporary but general hush descended. Porson opened one eye and looked sourly at the man he had come half way across the world to save.

'What's a fool like you doing in a dump like this?' he snarled.

# 10

The Select Committee on Liturgical Vestments was permeated by a covert and growing unease. Cardinal Chingada, poor man, was *particularly* uneasy.

Some weeks earlier, at the close of a perfectly routine session, Polenta had made an Announcement.

'Gentlemen,' he had said. 'I have Good News for you.'

The Cardinals, who had been fiddling with their briefcases, under the impression that the meeting was at an end, suddenly sat very still indeed. Unscheduled pieces of good news were far from popular with the Committee. The last occasion had signalled the 're-assignment' of Cardinal Feuchtwanger and he had not been heard of since.

'Good news,' Polenta repeated. He swept a glance like a wire brush along the rigid faces around the table. Balai-Rose felt the muscles at the back of his knees begin to twitch.

'The time is . . . ?' Instead of finishing the sentence he brought to bear a look of ferocious interrogation on Cardinal Fegato.

Fegato looked nervously at his watch.

'Ripe!' finished Polenta triumphantly, just as Fegato was getting his mouth open. 'Is it not . . . ?' (keeping his armour-piercing eyes on Fegato until Fegato had his mouth open again then switching them suddenly through ninety degrees) 'Cardinal MENSCHMEYER?'

Menschemeyer took the full impact of a salvo delivered over open sights almost without flinching.

'ROTTEN RIPE!' cried Polenta, drowning Menschmeyer's reply. 'So! No more delays. No more fence-sitting. No more PUSSYFOOTING. We are going to initiate . . . as from now . . .' (dramatic pause) 'Project NEW BROOM.'

No one moved. They waited for whatever was coming next. The brass tacks.

There were no brass tacks. Polenta picked up his papers and strode towards the door.

'So get busy!' he snapped over his shoulder as he disappeared from the room.

The meeting broke up in a state of subdued panic.

Since then, New Broom had come to occupy progressively more of each day's schedule, so that the normal pattern of business—what Balai-Rose called Procedural Routine—was nibbled away until it seemed likely to disappear without trace. Meetings came to be dominated by long hortatory speeches from the Chair concerning the havoc New Broom was expected to wreak in the ranks of the Enemy. Larding his remarks with a wealth of apposite quotations from the Book of Revelations, the 'Malleus Maleficorum', 'Mein Kampf', the posthumous memoirs of J. Edgard Hoover, the 'Summa Contra Haereses', and a selection of fiery passages from the Christian Fathers, Polenta let it be known that the forces of darkness were for it hot and strong this time. In the preparation and execution of this coup he relied on the fullest support from each and every member of the Committee and their various bureaux. Their finest hour was near. They were, he knew, straining at the leash to deliver the final crushing blast of the trumpet against the tents of the Midianites. After so many years of devoted struggle against subversion from within, without, above and below, it only required one last mighty effort and they would reap the reward of what had for so long been a thankless and covert struggle, etc. etc.

It was stirring stuff. But it increased rather than diminished the Uncertainty which, like a rabid mole, was mining away at the very foundations of the Cardinals' morale.

The root of the trouble lay in the fact that despite the length, number, and enthusiasm of Polenta's harangues, there remained a certain vagueness about the more concrete aspects of the operation. Details such as Timing, Targets, Logistics, Personnel and Tactical Methods had been only briefly touched on, if at all. Thus, while the 'Why?' of the business, and even to some extent the 'What?' were clear enough, the 'How?' 'Where?' 'When?' and 'Who?' of it remained shrouded in a fog of generalities.

The worst of it was that there was something in the way Polenta *assumed* their informed co-operation in his Great Matter which precluded questions; at the same time it prevented any of them from voicing to his fellows these petty but fundamental uncertainties. After the first day it was already too late. Now it was unthinkable.

Each of the Cardinals, isolated in his private bubble of disquiet, rose to the emergency as best he could. Theirs not to reason why; theirs to comply.

Menschmeyer scored ten points by opening the game with a massive report on the Liaison Situation with, as he said, special reference to New Broom. Fegato, with characteristic subtlety, dodged the necessity for an original contribution by firing off a whole series of counter-reports querying the reliability of Menschmeyer's agents, the efficacy of his tactics, and—rather daringly—their relevance to New Broom. Balai-Rose, no less expert than Fegato in producing a smoke-screen disguised as a firework display, submitted a daily Security Digest which grew increasing lurid as he sensed H-hour to be approaching.

Chingada, as Director of Plans, was furthest out on the highest limb. Polenta had made it plain that he looked to him to shoulder the main burden of detailed planning. After several days of fevered temporising, during which he had tried and failed to pick up some clue to what was happening from the submissions of his colleagues, Chingada had developed a feeling in his water that it was vain to look for help from his colleagues as they furtively expected the same service from him. So finally Chingada had announced:

   i. that a blow-by-blow operational plan, provisionally code-named 'Snow White' (in deference to Polenta's well-known colour-bias) was Pending if not Imminent;

  ii. that in the meantime he begged leave to submit a number of Contingency Plans. These dealt with aspects of New Broom which, while (admittedly) incidental to the main area of operations, were nevertheless (he ventured to suggest) a vital part of any scheme which claimed to be—and New Broom (it went without saying) could claim no less—one hundred percent Full and Final.

Then he went on to outline a series of extraordinary measures designed to counter putative mishaps to Snow White or any part thereof. They included:

—a plan for flooding the Pontine Marches;

—a plan for arming the Opus Dei;

—an alternative plan for neutralising the Opus Dei by interning them in Trappist monasteries;

—a plan for evacuating the Holy See by submarine;

—a plan for wrecking the Yugoslav tourist industry by filling the seas around Dubrovnik with portugese men-o'war floated over from Italy on a favourable wind;

—finally, a plan for using the Swiss Guard to seize the Vatican Radio Station and the offices of the *Osservatore Romano*.

These plans all received favourable notice from the Chair and the rest of the Committee secretly applauded Chingada's Rococo ingenuity. Entering into the spirit of the game, Fegato and Menschmeyer unleashed a heated dispute relative to the last of the above-mentioned plans, each man laying claim to the loyalty of the Vatican armed forces. The argument had an unlooked-for success and lasted three days.

But now time was running out.

Chingada shared with the rest of the Committee the unspoken conviction that New Broom was in some way connected with the forthcoming Council. And if this was so, then with the Council only weeks away the time for fence-sitting and pussy-footing was indeed past. And though Chingada's fertile mind had far from exhausted the possibilities of Contingency Planning, the mood of the Committee was getting dangerously unstable. Before long they would be forced, in self-defence, to break into open clamour to be made party to the details of Plan Snow White; and if unsatisfied this clamour would speedily degenerate into a clamour for the hide of the Director of Plans.

Chingada had not worked under Polenta all these years without learning that a well-timed cry of 'Off with his head!' covers a multitude of sins.

In desperation Chingada made foxy attempts to pump the other members of the Committee for anything they knew about New Broom. Failing that, he might at least trap one of them into admitting himself as much in the dark as anyone else. As a last-ditch play Chingada then would be able to use such an admission as a basis for the 'off-with-his-head' gambit.

He decided to concentrate on Balai-Rose, feeling he would be an easier nut to crack.

'This New Broom . . .' he said to Balai-Rose over coffee one day. His tone was carefully fraught with any number of different possible interpretations.

'Ah!' said Balai-Rose, enigmatically. And to himself, 'Je connais la musique, va!' He had already had the same conversation twice that week, once with Fegato and once with Menschmeyer.

There was a pause, the pregnant variety, and then Balai-Rose said, 'Ah!' again with even less emphasis than before. Parturiunt montes.

'It's going pretty well, don't you think?' said Chingada at last, eyeing the Frenchman narrowly from the shelter of his coffee-cup.

Balai-Rose went through a series of shrugs which might have signified anything at all, even an itchy shoulder blade.

Chingada said, 'Hmm, New Broom, yes . . .' and added some shrugs of his own.

There was a further pause during which Chingada quested hither and thither in the recesses of his mind for a better ploy and Balai-Rose cleaned out his ear with an end of the silver cross on his rosary.

Chingada decided to go for broke.

'It's playing hell with Procedural Routine,' he said.

He had touched a nerve. Balai-Rose had a full share of the Frenchman's love for order and precision.

'You are right!' he exclaimed with sudden fervour. 'A system so perfect! To be abandoned like an old rag!' But then, his eyes meeting those of Chingada, in ambush behind their coffee-cup, he broke off and added hastily: 'It is, of course, inevitable. Of the essence. The exigencies of the situation . . .'

'Of course,' said Chingada. And added suggestively, 'Alas . . .' But Balai-Rose had begun shrugging again and Chingada, realising he was getting nowhere, put down his coffee-cup and wandered away.

That left him only one card to play, and he hadn't been dealt it yet: a diversion. A big one, massive. A red herring in the fifty-megaton range. Nothing less would answer. . . .

And it was that very same day that, reading the reports from Sector Four, he had his first glimpse of light at the end of the tunnel. '. . . bigger than the Dead Sea Scrolls . . .' he read. That was magnitude for you. With growing excitement he read on. The Q-text! Yes, it might do.

Late into the night he laboured in a barely-controlled frenzy among the musty, paper-stuffed warrens of the Vatican archives. By morning he was ready, his evidence collected, his case prepared. It only remained to present the Chairman with the facts.

He decided not to wait for the morning's meeting. It was all or nothing. And now.

His purple robes flapping in the early morning breeze, his face grey with strain, he headed for the men's toilet in the north-west corner of the Borgia Court. The nature of his errand, he hoped, would justify his use of the emergency entrance to the bunker HQ.

Behind the locked door of the third cubicle from the left he muttered a hasty prayer to the Virgin of Guadalupe and pulled the chain.

# II

One fine morning a message appeared on Father MacCord's desk:

43935/8
*From*: DIRECTOR OF PLANS.
*To*: REV HEAD OF FIELD OPERATIONS.
*Sector*: FOUR.
*Date*: AS POSTMARK.
REF OUR 37201/4 ACKNOWLEDGING YOUR ACKNOWLEDGEMENT OF OUR 28033/2 INQUIRING ABOUT YOUR FAILURE TO ACKNOWLEDGE OUR QUERY 14952/2 REGARDING DELAY IN COMPLETION DATE ON CONTRACT NUMBER 688/6.
THIS CONTRACT IS WITHDRAWN AS FROM RECEIPT OF THIS ORDER.
ACKNOWLEDGE SOONEST.
IN NOM. P. F. ET. S.S.

Communications of this sort were everyday matters to Father James Eustace Eugene MacCord. On his shoulders rested the whole responsibility for the activities of the Service in the misty northern islands known to HQ as Sector Four and to the world at large as Great Britain.

He read the missive with the care he habitually gave to the minutiae of his work, however numerous. He inferred, from the style as much as from the contents, that the matter was urgent. He pressed a button on his desk and said to it: 'Rowena, my dear, send Seamus to me this instant.'

Seamus appeared as if rubbed from a lamp, massive in his black elastic-sided boots. MacCord gave him the message without a word. Seamus empocketed it and left. He drove across London and presented himself at an unremarkable house in an unremarkable street in the general area of Chiswick. Here, after duly enacting certain procedures which Seamus personally considered time-wasting and futile, he handed over the message and went away.

The whole operation went like clockwork. That is how Mac-Cord liked his operations to go.


# 12


Porson spent the afternoon pumping Fat-ass Niko on the document situation. It was done without finesse. Porson was in a hurry.

If you ask a Greek a question, he will tend to give you, not the answer which fits the facts as he knows them, but the answer which he thinks will make you happy. This is not done out of contempt for truth but from the desire to give pleasure.

It took Mr Kolofouskomenos about seven seconds to realise that Porson *wanted* there to be documents at the monastery, preferably in large numbers, and the older the better.

PORSON: (*taking Niko aside and poking an interrogative fore-finger into the Greek's fat belly*) Listen. . . . Did the old fool say anything about . . . documents . . . while he's been here? Eh?

NIKO: (*wide-eyed*) Documents? Hm.

PORSON: Documents, scrolls, manuscripts, pa-pie-rus-is, o l d p a p e r s.

NIKO: Ah! *Old* papers.

PORSON: Yes. Yes. Yes. Yes.

NIKO: You want to know did he *say* something about—?

PORSON: Well did he have any with him when he came?

NIKO: (*carefully*) Nooo. . . .

PORSON: So they're still at the stinking monastery then?

NIKO: Mr Porson, I can see it's no use to try to hide something from a man like you. Listen . . . (*conspiratorial glance*) why we don't go somewhere where we can talk?

And he took Porson outside and Told All.

It is doubtful whether the Photographer knew what was afoot. When he was not taking pictures or piloting the helicopter (his other function) he was as if switched off. He just sat and looked at his hands. He was perhaps the nearest thing to a machine-for-living that human evolution has so far achieved.

After supper that night they sat on Niko's veranda drinking what he called cognac, in reality raki of the vilest sort made from a mash of dates and millet.

'The reason it's painted orange,' Porson was saying in answer to a query from Mrs Kolofouskomenou, 'is to enable the stinking thing to be spotted if it falls down in the stinking desert or the stinking jungle and they send another of the stinkers to look for it.'

Porson's temper hadn't improved since his arrival.

'Will it take three?' Flake asked.

'Yes,' said the Photographer, not looking up from his hands which were lying spread out in front of him on the table.

'I come too,' said Fat-ass Niko.

'Too heavy,' said the Photographer.

Mrs Kolofouskomenou had her hands under the table and was doing something on her knee.

'He can have my place,' said Flake. 'I'm not all that keen to go back there really. They might. . . . I might. . . .'

'You come too,' said Porson. 'We need you.'

'We don't need him,' said the Photographer, pointing with his head towards Fat-ass Niko.

'Mpf!' said Porson.

'But!' cried Fat-ass Niko. 'The other things.'

'We'll talk about them when we get back,' said Porson.

'But!'

'My God!' cried Flake involuntarily. He had just unfolded the note which Mrs Kolofouskomenou had slid under his glass while he was looking the other way. It read—

Beware!

They took off next morning at dawn and followed the river upstream. The helicopter carried Porson, Flake and the Photographer. Fat-ass Niko had been left behind despite his protests. It had been physically impossible to fit him into the machine.

They followed the river upstream.

Flake was withdrawn, moody. Porson was semi-prostrate, the 'cognac' having done nothing for his headache. Before take-off he had—speaking between the clenched teeth of a man at the limits of suffering—outlined the purpose of the trip: to collect 'stinking copy' and some 'stinking pictures' and subsequently to 'get the hell out of this putrid hole'.

The Photographer, too, was even more taciturn than usual. He was puzzling over a note he had found lying on the pilot's seat when he boarded the aircraft and which said—

Of what?

# 13

24, Willow Crescent, Chiswick, served as a forward command post in Father MacCord's sector of the far-flung battle zone. The house was under the direction of one Felix, in whose person were combined a number of functions, all indispensable to the day-to-day running of the organisation.

Primary among these functions was that of Signals Officer. It was, accordingly, on Felix's desk that Order Number 43935/8 now lay—together, let it be said, with a staggering quantity of similar messages. The room was full of paper.

Felix's whole office was a vast 'In' tray.

Not many days after the arrival of Order Number 43935/8, Seamus happened to find himself in Felix's office with time heavy on his hands. He sat in the office chair with his feet (size 13) on the office desk. Felix was absent on a mission, namely the return of a round number of empty Guinness bottles to the off-licence.

The room was quiet. From time to time a car would be heard passing in the street outside.

It was raining in Chiswick, as it was elsewhere in London.

Highpockets stood by the window, biting his nails and squinting mournfully up at a dingy sky from which a dingy light filtered down to the dingy streets below. The window admitted a ration of this light sufficient to reveal or create indoors an atmosphere in harmony with that currently prevailing outside, to wit: a dingy atmosphere.

'It's bloody raining again,' said Highpockets.

Highpockets, as his name implies, was as small, sour and weedy as his partner Seamus was large, florid and benign. His voice had a peevish whine to it which betrayed his Cockney origins. Seamus, on the other hand, came from County Kerry of respectable middle-class stock (his father a demented pot-house keeper, his mother a witch of some reputation locally) and his speech had all the rich overtones of methane bubbles in a peat bog. Seamus had early been destined for a career in the legal profession and had in fact joined the Gardai at the age of nineteen, but after a few years had resigned (for religious reasons) to take up his present occupation.

Both men, as if to emphasise discrepancies in physique and personality, wore identical working clothes—double-breasted suits with padded shoulders, dark grey in colour, and for walking out, black bowlers with fawn trenchcoats. Seamus wore a conservative twenty-four-inch trouser bottom; Highpockets favoured the avant-garde idiom—sixteen inches.

Despite an undeniable hint of broad comedy in the common front they presented to the world, Seamus and Highpockets formed an efficient—on occasion deadly efficient—team which enjoyed high esteem in professional circles.

'Would you have an unconquerable aversion to sitting down here and having a hand of brag with your old friend?' inquired Seamus.

'Bloody rain.'

Seamus winced. He had signed the pledge and never swore. The most he would permit himself was a coy 'Feck!' in moments of unusual crisis.

'These islands of ours enjoy a climate whose temperateness is the wonder and envy of heathen nations,' he said. 'Did no one ever tell you that?'

'That's the one where you got seven cards and tries to get rid of them.'

'It is not. And haven't I explained the rules to you a thousand times and more?'

Seamus had an aversion to using a declarative sentence when an interrogative would serve.

'And changed them every bleeding time,' said Highpockets.

'It's because you're confused in your mind that you think so,' said Seamus smoothly. 'Isn't it just a way I have of making things EASIER for you? Come and sit down here now.'

'This rain,' said Highpockets, approaching. 'And me going on me holidays next week. What the hell is these papers doing here?'

'Terow them on the floor man. Clear away a space there. What's it to be, Broadstairs again?'

'I got an auntie there runs a boarding house, don't I?'

'I'm sure you have. Will I deal now?'

'Look at all this bloody rubbish for Christ's sake,' said Highpockets as he swept quires of multi-coloured onionskin message forms off the spare chair.

'Information,' Seamus assured him, riffling a pack of dog-eared cards, 'is surely to be reckoned the very lifesblood of an organisation like ours. As it is of any system of human relationships. Isn't it orders, reports and memurandums that keeps the very wheels of the Service turning? Did you never stop to think of that?'

Highpockets gave a cry of exasperation.

'There's JAM on these papers! Some filthy bastard has been spreading jam all over them. Look at me hands. I got bloody jam all over them.'

'It will be Felix again,' said Seamus. 'He has no conception of Christian cleanliness, that Felix, and is known for a terrible man when he is eating. That is your intellectuals for you. Haven't I seen him take a pork chop from his plate and put it in his pocket the way it was a box of matches?'

'What the hell am I going to do with this lot then?'

'There is a trick to these things,' said Seamus, 'known as Office Procedure.' He considered the problem for a moment and then said in a tone of decision: 'We will file the whole lot under R.'

'How's that?'

'Watch me now,' said Seamus. And with a masterful sweep of his forearm he cleared half the contents of the desk-top into the waste-paper basket. 'That is how it is done,' he said. 'R for rubbish.'

Order Number 43935/8 had come to the end of the line.

'I hope you know what you're doing, mate,' said Highpockets. A worrier.

'Would I be doing it if I didn't?' answered Seamus with simple logic.

'He'll miss them, won't he? What happens then?'

Seamus looked at him pityingly.

'My poor man,' he said, 'did you imagine in your ignorance there wouldn't be COPIES of every one of them papers right here in this same office?'

'I just hope you're right, that's all.'

'Office Procedure,' said Seamus. 'Go and wash now. And for the love of God let us have a hand of cards and a little peace.'

# 14

Rasselas was down by the river taking stones out of the fish trap. The noise of the helicopter's approach was lost in the noise of the water and when he first heard it and looked up, it was already overhead. He saw it begin to slide down an invisible incline towards the village.

He began to run.

He reached the edge of the village on one side as the helicopter lowered itself to the ground on the other.

Among the houses chaos had broken out. Alerted by the clatter of the machine the monks had poured from their huts like a horde of cockroaches and were rushing about in various directions, waving their hands and uttering excited cries. Some, under the impression that the Second Coming of the Blessed Shn'ut—long supposed to be imminent—was upon them, made rapidly for the landing spot. Others, particularly those of a more doomy stamp, had leapt to the conclusion that the Day of Judgement was in progress and had decided to give the event a wide berth, hoping their absence would go unremarked. A third group were wrestling with the cattle, who had gone mad, broken down the thorn hedges and were savaging the mealies. This profusion of conflicting goals led to repeated collisions among the individuals composing the mass. Hypertrophy of the adrenal cortices reached epidemic proportions. Mass trauma loomed. The church bell began tolling desperately.

Dodging and weaving, Rasselas arrived unharmed at the far side of the village and joined a group of monks—some bewildered, some ecstatic—who were waiting on the outcome from a respectful distance.

The shattering noise of the machine died into a whine, a few coughs, and then silence. The dust began to settle. Those of the monks who had thrown themselves face down on the ground rose uncertainly to their knees. Those on their knees rose to their feet. The yelling from the houses behind gave place to a doubt-filled quiet. The church bell stopped.

The door of the helicopter opened and Flake stepped out.

The monks looked at each other. Sheepish smiles began to pass to and fro among them. The word spread back to the village. The casualties of the mêlée struggled upright, shaking the dust from their robes and picking bits of cow-dung from their beards. Those who had sought sanctuary in the church peeped out.

Rasselas hugged the Professor in his little arms. His face was a smile entirely surrounded by hair. 'Tiffin-time,' he said, still panting, 'you have come back to us.'

And the Professor smiled too and said: 'How do you like *my* miracle?'

There was no musketry, there being no muskets.

# 15

In Cardinal Polenta's organisation, the process by which decisions taken at command level were translated into operational terms and forwarded to the front line embodied in tactical directives was one of amazing complexity. There was nothing inherently improbable in the fact that the decision to annihilate an anomaly in Sector Four, embodied in Contract Number 6886, was ultimately incarnated in the person of a blind and toothless beggar named Qu'at. In a system so harassed by its own entropy things could hardly have turned out otherwise.

Qu'at was seated on the steps leading to the front porch of the house of Mr Nikos Kolofouskomenos, merchant, of Famaka.

Famaka, by the way, was not in Sector Four but in Sector Six. That's how things were.

At intervals during the day Mrs Kolofouskomenou had made several attempts to dislodge the beggar Qu'at. These onsets had achieved nothing. Qu'at had every intention of staying where he was until he had done what he came to do. His pay-packet was at stake. What the houseproud Mrs Kolofouskomenou regarded as a noisome eyesore was in reality a walking case-history in classical economics, living proof of the power of the profit-motive.

The master of the house, as Qu'at knew, was not at home. Disgruntled at his exclusion from Porson's raiding party, Niko had sought solace in the sudorific embraces of Choula, his mistress. This was a mammoth lady, of mixed Armenian and Somali extraction, who Niko had installed together with a correspondingly gigantic brass bed in a tiny one-roomed love nest on the outskirts of town. Choula was as fat, easy-going and juicy as the lawful Mrs K. was thin, sour and shrivelled. Niko called her his 'water-melon' and his 'little red mullet' and, to preserve her girlish figure, kept her strictly to a high-calory diet of milk and sweet potatoes.

Qu'at was apprised of Niko's whereabouts by an intelligence source he had no reason to regard as anything but infallible. On form, Niko wouldn't be back until the evening, if then.

Qu'at waited.

He carried, in addition to his begging bowl, a stick or cane such as forms part of the standard tackle of persons of his vocation and disability. It was about four feet long and varied in diameter between an inch and an inch and a half, or there-abouts.

He sat on the steps through the heat of the day and neither moved nor spoke. His indifference to his environment would have seemed, even to a close observer, total. He ignored the customers passing up and down the steps. He ignored the inter-mittent offensives launched against him, both orally and with the business end of a broom, by Mrs Kolofouskomenou. He ignored the flies which clustered round his pus-caked eyelids. He didn't even beg. He waited.

# 16

The photographer lay in the cabin of the helicopter, curled up on the floor. His head rested on a wooden box which bore the stencilled instruction—

STORE IN A COOL PLACE OTHER SIDE UP.

The cabin door stood open. The interior was lit by an unsteady glow from the fires which had been lit in a circle round the machine. The fires were dying now and the monks who had built and tended them had drifted away one by one to their hard beds.

In only one of the huts a light still burned where Rasselas and his friend the Professor sat talking, talking, among the bloody dishes and overturned cups.

It had been a great feast that night in the village.

Among the houses moved a thin and furtive shadow, casting suspicious glances to left and to right, making for the church.

# 17

After their night at the monastery, Porson and party reached Famaka the next morning in time for lunch. Porson was in good humour during the trip, as he had reason to be.

Immediately after the meal, at 12.37 local time, occurred the sad death of Mr Kolofouskomenos.

The authorities were soon on the scene in the shape of a diminutive police sergeant with a fez stuck miraculously to one side of his head. He was accompanied by an interpreter. Eager to get at the facts, they proceeded to a verbal examination of the witnesses. By and large the deponents were unanimous in their accounts: during the meal relations between the dead man and Mr Porson had been strained; afterwards Mr Porson had retired to the veranda with a bottle (soda water, in his version) and Mr Kolofouskomenos had followed him out; those still in the house had then heard voices raised in dispute; this appeared to concern the equitable division of profits accruing from a common business venture (according to Porson, a bet); then Mr Porson had re-entered the room 'shouting and waving his arms'; seconds later had appeared in the open doorway the figure of Mr Kolofouskomenos, swaying on his feet, with a small hole in his chest and a very large one in his back; he had then died without naming his aggressor.

Having collected these depositions the forces of law and order retired to Police Headquarters to decide who to arrest. There was hot discussion before, by a majority vote, Porson was nominated. The feeling was that he, of all the contenders for the post, would best be able to support the legal costs of pro-longed imprisonment without trial; his possession of his own private helicopter, gaily painted, was impressive evidence of the resources of his employers. It was further agreed that Her Brittanic Majesty would hardly risk the loss of face involved should one of her subjects be left to languish in a filthy jail (the jail in Famaka was very filthy) for lack of a few quid in the proper quarters.

Porson was accordingly placed in carcere et vinculis, deprived of alcohol, and left to sweat.

Flake and the Photographer, after a few formalities, quite expensive, were told they were free to leave and left.

Meanwhile the blind beggar Qu'at was no longer around. No one had thought to ask him his version of the crime. If they had, he might have seen fit to reveal that his innocent-seeming stick concealed a custom-built single-shot 7·62 mm gas rifle of Italian manufacture, firing a high-velocity soft-nosed bullet with considerable accuracy at ranges of up to seventy-five feet.

When the news of Fat Niko's murder reached the Embassy in Khartoum it caused no excitement whatever among the secretaries and coding clerks in the chancery. It was thought, however, that the Ambassador ought to be informed and a PPA was despatched to put His Excellency in the picture.

His Excellency was at breakfast.

'Porson? Porson?' he said through his toast and marmalade. 'Who's he when he's at home? Eh?'

'The Famaka thing, sir. You may remember we—'

'Ah!' said His Excellency. 'That newspaper chappie. Serve him right. Never does to go sticking your nose into local politics. . . . (chomp, chomp) The fuzzies don't like it. Not the thing.'

'Quite so, sir. And . . . what action do you suggest?'

'Action? Disown the feller of course. And be quick about it. . . . Who'd he do in anyhow?'

'A Greek, sir.'

'Hah! A Greek. Might have known it. A damn shifty lot I've always said.'

The PPA coughed discreetly. 'Of course, sir. But this *particular* Greek, Kolo . . . Kolo . . . Kolo-somethingorother . . . It seems he's our . . . ah . . . consul down there.'

His Excellency choked on his toast and the veins on his nose began to flare up.

'Consul!' he cried. 'H.M. or British?'

'Oh, British, British. If you remember, sir, we thought—'

'Oof!' said His Excellency. 'That's all right then.'

But when the PPA was half way to the door, His Excellency stopped him with an afterthought.

'While you're about it . . . (munch) you might as well disown the Greek chappie. Two birds with one stone and so forth.'

His Excellency went back to the cricket scores in the airmail edition of the 'Times' and the PPA hied him back to the Chancery to set about disowning the defunct consul and his slayer. The work of a moment.

Let it not be said that H.M.G. has lost the capacity to act fast in a crisis.

*Part Two*

CRANLEY HEAVENSPUR

# I

'LadiesandgentlemenwehavejustlandedatLondonAirportHeathro-
witisfouroclocklocaltimetheexternaltemperatureiseightdegreesce-
ntigradeerererdegreesfarenheitwillyoupleasekeepyourseatbeltsfa-
steneduntiltheplanecomestoacompletestopwehopeyouhavehadap-
leasantflightandlookforwardtowelcomingyouonboardagainsoon,'
said the Stewardess in three languages, smiling tiredly into
her hand mike.

Professor Flake turned to the Arab gentleman seated next to
him.

'Good to be home again, eh?'

The Arab didn't answer. He had his nose pressed to the
window and was staring out wildly trying to get a fix on Mecca.

The Professor fingered his chin. He didn't like these long night
flights. You arrived with a bad taste in your mouth and needing
a shave. He had slept badly. There was something on his mind.
Just before leaving Khartoum he had discovered the reliquary in
his luggage, wrapped in a shirt. He had said nothing about it,
not even to the Photographer, who had accompanied him as far
as Cairo before taking a separate plane home and leaving Flake
to spend a blissful few days measuring the Great Pyramid. In
many ways the Professor was nobody's old fool: he had a
shrewd idea of how the thing had got into his wardrobe since
he recognised the shirt it was wrapped in as Porson's. But he

had no intention of letting the Photographer claim it for his paper on Porson's behalf. It posed certain problems though. How was he going to explain to the Customs the presence in his luggage of the mummified and jewel-encrusted virile member of a thousand-year-dead Coptic saint?

The plane emitted fifty or sixty urgent-looking Levantines plus a similar number of American tourists whose cameras were bursting with hard-won footage of the Aswan Dam and the swimming pool of the Nile Hilton (though many of them had no idea which was which).

The passengers had to make their way through a crowd of reporters buzzing and clustering round the exit steps like flies round a dead mule. Rain streaked across the dark glasses of the Arabs and the blue-rinsed hair of the American ladies as they shouldered their way across the tarmac and filed up the ramp.

The Stewardess held the Professor back until the others were out. He emerged blinking into a maelstrom of flashbulbs and microphones. The steps wobbled crazily under the pressure of the stampeding newsfiends.

'Professor!' yelled the reporters. 'A word in our ears! . . . A few words! . . . The scroll! . . . Can you tell us? . . . The Q text! . . . It is true? . . .'

The Professor peered down at them. What on earth were they gabbling about? The Stewardess stood beside him and looked on indulgently.

'A statement! A statement!' twittered the mob.

Professor Flake held up his hands for silence in a magisterial gesture. The shouting ebbed. Pencils hung poised over half a hundred notebooks. Microphones waved towards him like a snake-pit at feeding time. A frown crossed his face as he searched his mind for something to fit the occasion. Then he had an Inspiration.

'No comment,' he said, beaming.

# 2

'But we can't just leave him there to rot,' said the Features Editor.

'Oh can't we?' said the Editor, with a snarl in his voice. 'Give me one reason why not.'

# 3

Father MacCord in a green three-piece tweed travelling suit was lurking behind a pillar in the Arrival Building at London Airport. He hung around long enough to make sure that the system of tails he had attached to the Professor was working smoothly. Then he took the first plane for Rome.

In the Via Adolfo Muni, just off St Peter's Square, he went into a *pasticceria* and ordered a specific quantity of *lasagna verde*. Three and a half minutes later he was duly being admitted to the Situations Room in Polenta's HQ.

He found Cardinal Chingada in a side room behind a door marked DIRECTOR OF PLANS in swashbuckling red letters. Chingada was up to his ears in work. The desk at which he sat was piled so high with books and papers that he himself was all but invisible, and a stream of assistants hurried in and out with little trolleys of new material from the Library or the Archives.

Chingada didn't bother to explain to MacCord what he was doing. The fewer people that knew, the stronger his own position. At the Committee Meeting that morning Polenta, acting on Chingada's information, had announced that in view of a threat to Security from an Unexpected Quarter, New Broom was temporarily suspended 'pending clarification'. This announcement, while it had a visibly crumpling effect on the morale of Chingada's colleagues, left Chingada himself feeling better than he had done for a long time. The piquancy of being the only member of the Committee in full possession of the facts had largely restored his zest for living. He took a proprietary view of the emergency (nothing more natural since it was he who had invented it) and meant to extract the maximum of moral advantage from the ill-concealed bewilderment of Cardinals Menschmeyer, Fegato and Balai-Rose. He felt no obligation to give them any explanation for his sudden frenzied interest in the Oxyrhynchus fragments, the 'Sayings of Jesus', the 'Pistis Sophia' and the Qumran scrolls.

He heard MacCord's report, asked a few pertinent questions, and dismissed him.

A little disconsolate, MacCord made his way out through the *pasticceria*, parked his *lasagna* in a convenient dustbin and took a taxi back to the air terminal.

Chingada hurried to Father Singleton with a digest of Mac-Cord's report.

Singleton in his turn hurried to Polenta with a digest of Chingada's digest of MacCord's report.

So much digestion inevitably had a transmogrifying effect on the report itself. In the process of re-transmission each man subtly and subconsciously adjusted the facts as he heard them to the situation as he saw it. The process was cumulative: in the twenty minutes or so that elapsed between MacCord's interview with Chingada and Singleton's with Polenta the urgency of the situation increased by a factor of three.

Singleton found Polenta in a smouldering condition. The sudden intervention of a new factor at the very moment when his schemes were so close to fruition was one more instance of the diabolical perversity of the enemies who beset his path. But, far from discouraging him, this new machination of his omni-present adversaries merely added fuel to his burning resolve. . . .

As he listened in silence to Singleton's report, his eyes glowed, and his fingers slid lovingly over the burnished occiput of the human skull that sat among the telephones on his desk.

Behind him on the wall, framed, his favourite quotation:

KILL THEM ALL
GOD WILL RECOGNISE HIS OWN

When Singleton had finished there was a long silence. Suddenly Polenta barked: 'Well?'

'Your Eminence?'

'Well—who does he think he's fooling?'

'Haha, yes, quite so.'

'Well who?'

Singleton was taken aback. 'Well . . . no one, Your Eminence?'

'Wrong! Me. That's who he thinks he's fooling. Me.'

'How so, Your Eminence?' asked Singleton warily.

'The facts, man,' rapped Polenta impatiently. 'Look at the facts.' He ticked them off on his fingers. 'One—he's gone to ground, holed up. Two—he refuses to make any statements to the press, not a word about the document, nothing. Why?'

'I . . . don't know . . . perhaps—'

'Because he's clever, that's why. But not clever enough. And the press know, of course.'

'There have been . . . rumours,' said Singleton, very cautious now. 'Nothing definite.'

'You see?' said Polenta triumphantly. 'Oh they're sly, that lot. Biters. But they know all right. And I know they know. They don't fool me, Singleton. *They're sitting on it.*'

He mused for a time. Singleton stayed tense. A muscle in his cheek was beginning to twitch.

'In the house?' asked Polenta, returning to his muttons.

'We have someone inside, Your Eminence.'

'Reliable?'

'Oh, perfectly.'

'*No one* is reliable, Singleton, remember that. . . . In the country you said? Barricaded?'

'Well . . . incommunicado.'

'Right, barricaded. . . . It's pathetic, Singleton. Who does he think he's dealing with, Boy Scouts?'

The Cardinal got up and crossed to a map of Europe on the

wall. He eyed it moodily up and down and then made a lightning jab which brought a splayed finger-tip down squarely and hard on Greater London, crushing it like an insect.

'MacCord,' said Singleton.

Polenta rounded on him with an eyebrow cocked into a question mark.

'A good man, Your Eminence. One of the best.'

A long silence again.

'Paper Bag?' cried Polenta.

It was Singleton's turn to raise an interrogative eyebrow.

'Code name for this operation. I want a plan on my desk within the hour. When it's ready you'll go to London yourself and help MacCord get it off the ground. And no fumbles. With something this big the effects of a mistake would be . . . ?'

'Incalculable,' supplied Singleton with his fingers crossed.

'Right,' said Polenta. 'That's all. Now move.'

As Singleton bent low over the desk to kiss the ring extended to him, he found himself staring upside-down into the empty sockets of the Cardinal's memento mori.

'And remember, Singleton,' said Polenta when Singleton had his hand on the door.

Singleton turned.

'Of course, Your Eminence.'

'Well what, man, what?'

'Er . . . no one is reliable, Your Eminence?'

'TIME, Singleton, TIME.'

Outside, Singleton felt like a man who has just walked blindfold through a minefield.

Polenta watched on a television screen Singleton's back disappearing down a corridor. Suddenly he picked up a pen and scribbled a note on a pad:

> Singleton sweats too much.
> Investigate.

He looked hard at what he had written and then underlined the whole thing three times. Then he went back to work.

He had reached S for Socinians.

Two days later, Father MacCord's mother in Tunbridge Wells found a postcard with an Italian stamp among her mail. It was a picture of the Colosseum, morbidly coloured. The caption on the back ('Rome—View of the Colosseum' in four languages with numerous inaccuracies) had been scratched out and replaced with the words SOMEWHERE IN ITALY. It was unsigned.

# 4

Cranley Heavenspur swung down from the bus in Victoria Street while it was still moving and reeled along the pavement towards his place of work. He kept his eyes shut and cursed the malevolence of an evolutionary mechanism which had failed to provide human beings with ear-lids. The vicious roar of the traffic and the clenched faces of a million, scurrying, clock-crazed wage earners made him feel sick and weak.

He paused for a second in front of the heavy Victorian façade of—

MULVANEY & TOON
ECCLESIASTICAL FURNISHERS
& CLERICAL OUTFITTERS
EST. 1897.

He took a deep breath, looked at his watch. Late. He went in.

'You're late, Heavenspur,' said Bayliss, raising his pimply face from his ledgers with a look of smug malevolence. 'Again.'

Cranley ignored him and walked straight past, heading for the door marked—

DEVOTIONAL ARTICLES. TRADE ONLY.

Bayliss waited till he had his hand on the doorknob.

'Oh, Heavenspur,' he said sweetly. 'Father MacCord wishes to see you. In his office. At once, he said.'

Cranley turned from the door.

'Why?' he asked.

'I'm sure I couldn't tell you. But I suppose you could find out. If you go and ask him.'

Bayliss bent again over his desk. Cranley looked hard at Bayliss for a few moments. He hated him, for the good reason that Bayliss was a hateful person.

'LEMMING!' shouted Cranley as he turned and made for the stairs.

Bayliss heaved a fetid sigh of abused humility over his impeccable columns.

The offices were on the third floor.

'Ah, Heavenspur. Sit down.'

Father MacCord, clad in his usual hearty tweeds, stood with his back to the window, whirling his rosary and letting it wind itself round his extended forefinger, a process which gave rise to a constant series of whirs, rattles and clicks.

The office was large and gloomy, lit by a single small window. Previous experience rather than present perception led Cranley to posit a smile of the benign class on Father MacCord's red and circular countenance.

Cranley hunted round for a chair and when he found one, sat on it.

'Now then Heavenspur, I, ah, left word with young Bayliss that you were to come up the very moment you arrived. It is now . . .' (he glanced out of the window '. . . seventeen minutes past nine. We must, ah, suppose then that you either ignored my instruction or that you were, ah, late again. Again.'

MacCord's voice had a slightly grating, Capone-ish quality that belied the impression he would otherwise have given of a diminutive Friar Tuck. Also he had a curious habit of suddenly clamping his teeth shut in mid-sentence as if unwilling to relinquish the whole of an utterance without a struggle.

'My cat,' said Cranley desperately. He was still panting from the stairs and punch-drunk from the traumas incurred in getting from his bed to his place of work. 'Stamped to death. Found it this morning outside my house. Irishman. Drunk. I live in

68

Kilburn, you see. Had to arrange for the funeral. If you knew how I—'

He broke off. The thought of his beloved cat horribly done to death on his very doorstep between midnight and matins choked his eyes with tears and his throat with sobs.

'Ah,' said MacCord. 'Your pet. Your little friend. Flattened. An innocent victim of Celtic barbarism.'

'Barbarism,' said Cranley in a muffled voice.

'You have my sincere sympathy, Heavenspur,' said MacCord in tones of sincere sympathy. He knew perfectly well that Cranley neither had, nor ever had had, a cat. He had a dossier on Cranley a foot thick. 'Very well. We shall say no more, ah, about it. I shall content myself with reminding you that despite the, ah, spiritual connotations of our work here, we are first and foremost a business concern. We are out to make a profit.' He paused for a moment. 'A gigantic profit,' he added. 'Efficiency, ah, counts, Heavenspur. And punctuality is no small part of efficiency. Do I make myself clear?'

'Oh yes.'

'I'm, ah, glad to hear it.'

Cranley felt rather than saw the smile return to his superior's face. The r.p.m. of the rosary picked up a few notches.

'But there is another matter, Heavenspur. In fact the real reason for your, ah, visit.'

'If it's about the aspersions. . . .'

'It is not. It is about. . . . It is about. . . . Miss Thirkell!'

So that was it.

Miss Thirkell, since first she came to work for MacCord, had been the dogstar of all Cranley's daydream voyages in the world of high romance. There was an elusiveness, an aloofness, about her which fanned and fed Cranley's obsession. The root cause of the trouble was Miss Thirkell's breasts—the most tremendous pair of knockers Cranley had ever come across, a reality more wildly alluring than his wildest fantasies. These twin mountains of delight stood perpetually on the horizons of his life, always unattainable, yet always beckoning him on to impossible feats of exploration and conquest.

And yet his relations with Miss Thirkell had been . . . unsatisfactory. To say the least. The question was, how much did MacCord know? And who had told him?

'I have never laid a finger on Miss Thirkell, whose person is sacred to me,' asserted Cranley hotly.

'No one said you had, Heavenspur.'

'I have enemies in the shop. I demand to face my accusers.' Cranley began to wave his arms around.

'Perhaps, MacCord, I had better handle this.' A new voice, an unctuous, oily voice, spoke from a dark corner of the office behind Cranley's back, indicating a presence hitherto unsuspected.

Cranley cranked his head round to locate the source of the signal. A certain shuffling was heard and a lanky, black-clad, blue-chinned figure emerged from the shadows to stand by Cranley's chair.

'As you wish, Singleton,' said MacCord. And to Cranley he said: 'Heavenspur, this is Father Singleton. He has come over from, ah, head office, to help us with a few, ah, administrative problems. I might as well tell you that Father Singleton is already in the picture, Heavenspur, so I want you to answer his questions frankly and without any, ah . . .'

'Reservations,' said Singleton. 'Now then,' Singleton stood for a few moments with his hands clasped, staring thoughtfully at the top of Cranley's head.

'This is a sad business, Heavenspur,' he began. 'If half of what I hear is true. Now you say that you have never laid a finger on Miss Thirkell?'

'Never once.'

'Would you deny that you have laid . . . eyes . . . on her?'

'No.'

'And would you care to deny that this . . . laying-on of eyes, as it were, is normally accompanied by a certain, how shall we put it? . . . lusting on your part?'

'That's not fair!' cried Cranley. 'Someone has been slandering me. I demand—'

'Very well, very well,' interrupted Singleton smoothly, strok-

ing his chin. 'Let us set aside the question of the lusting . . .
for the moment . . . and pass to another matter. The matter of
the beeswax candle.'

'Aha!' exclaimed MacCord, dashing his beads from hand to
hand.

'Steady, James,' warned Singleton. 'Now, Heavenspur. . . .'

'An accident,' muttered Cranley. 'I was simply holding the
candle—'

'A huge candle!' cried MacCord.

'Yes, a big one. And I tripped on a monstrance or something.
It was dark and I couldn't see and Miss Thirkell was, well, in
the way, and we sort of, at least I did. If you don't believe me,
ask her.'

'Don't worry,' said Singleton. 'I shall. I intend to.' He paused
for a long moment. 'You have not explained what you were
doing in the altar bread room with a monstrance and a fourteen-
inch beeswax candle.'

'And Miss Thirkell,' put in MacCord.

'Quite. And Miss Thirkell,' agreed Singleton, licking his lips
quickly. 'Please restrain yourself, James.'

Cranley seemed to have deflated to half his normal size.

'Well, Heavenspur. I'm waiting. We're waiting. The explanation.'

'I love Miss Thirkell,' squeaked Cranley in a voice half its
normal size.

'Ha!' cried MacCord. 'You see?'

Singleton ignored him.

'And does Miss Thirkell reciprocate this . . . passion?' he
inquired with signs of strong interest.

'I . . . don't know.'

'Of course she doesn't,' said MacCord. 'She was in bed for
three days after the candle incident. Nervous collapse.'

'The incident was an accident,' protested Cranley, throwing
euphony to the winds.

'So you told us,' said Singleton in a musing, Jesuitical voice.
'So you told us. The fact remains that you forced your attentions on a female member of Father MacCord's staff in the

presence of the unsanctified Host. Thereby you imperilled the physical and mental well-being, not to mention the reputation, of a valued employee, and, at the same time, which is worse, *your immortal soul.*'

Cranley said nothing. He sat slumped in his chair, glaring at his feet as if about to pick a fight with them. Father Singleton crossed to the window where he and MacCord conferred briefly in undertones, like doctors in a sickroom. Then Singleton turned to Cranley.

'For the moment, Heavenspur, there is no more to be said. I shall of course be speaking to Miss Thirkell to get her side of the story before I make my . . . report.'

Cranley rose to his feet. Singleton walked him to the door, his arm round Cranley's shoulders. Suddenly he was all honey.

'I'm glad we've had this little chat . . .'

# 5

Mrs Trigger came downstairs with a tray on which was an empty mug marked 'Ovaltine'. It was the Professor's habit to woo Morpheus with cocoa.

She washed the mug carefully in the kitchen and put it away. Then she went to stand at the foot of the stairs and cocked an ear towards the Professor's bedroom. Snores could be heard. Satisfied, she crossed the hall in a swish of her stiff white apron until she stood by the study door. From the depths of her clothing she produced a key, opened the door carefully, switched on the light and went in, closing the door noiselessly behind her.

It says much for Father MacCord's efficiency that he had recruited Mrs Trigger several days *before* the return of the resuscitated Professor from Famaka. It was the most banal of human frailties that had placed her in his power. During the Professor's absence Mrs Trigger had contracted an illicit relationship with one Hawkins, the van driver employed by the local grocer. Hawkins, in fact, a spry sexagenarian despite his wooden leg, had over the years taken advantage of the mobility his occupation afforded to form a number of similar liaisons in the district.

How word of Mrs Trigger's fall had come to the ears of Father MacCord there is no knowing. Of course, the possibility of a Special Revelation cannot be ruled out. However this may be, MacCord had put his knowledge to work like a true pragmatist. Mrs Trigger had responded magnificently to the threat of Disclosure—with its corollaries: scandal, job-loss without reference, etc. Her initial hesitations overcome, she had proved a valuable operative. Her information was given an 'A' rating in London.

As an additional precaution, indicative of MacCord's thoroughness, Hawkins had been similarly and independently won over. Under the threat of a village-wide smear campaign he had been persuaded to file confidential reports on Mrs Trigger, thus raising their relationship to the status of a Network.

So elegant a system of checks and balances kept the status more or less quo in the Flake household. The Professor, ignorant of the storm of woefully divided loyalties raging beneath Mrs Trigger's starchy exoderm, continued to enjoy her careful housekeeping and excellent cuisine; MacCord enjoyed the services of a competent intelligence source; and Hawkins, with unabated vigour, enjoyed what was left every Tuesday and Friday.

Mrs Trigger sat now in the Professor's study at the Professor's desk, biting the end of her pencil and wrestling with her Problem.

Her instructions were: to submit a daily report on the Professor's progress with the decipherment of the manuscript. What manuscript? she had wanted to know. Why, the one he brought back from Africa, what else?

At this point Mrs Trigger was shrewd enough to realise that MacCord was in the grip of a powerful misconception; further, that a *true* account of the Professor's activities would not only be disbelieved, it would be positively unwelcome. She had therefore refrained from pointing out that, to her certain knowledge, the Professor had brought no manuscript back from Africa, or if he had, he certainly wasn't working on it. He spent most of the day in the bath, 'meditating' as he called it—a nasty foreign habit he seemed to have picked up on his travels.

She was left, then, with the problem of finding a suitable stand-in for the 'day-to-day working notes' she had been told to look for.

Her solution to the problem showed a rude brilliance which suggested that Mrs Trigger was wasted in the kitchen.

Every night she went to the study, selected at random any book from the Professor's extensive library in which the word 'manuscript' figured prominently, and copied out ten or twelve lines of it in a slow and sprawling hand.

This procedure had resulted in a stream of miscellaneous and wildly ill-assorted information on palaeography, carbon-14 dating, the use of diacritical marks in Palmyrene Cursive, thermoluminescence tests and the detection of palimpsests, which had more than satisfied MacCord's simple mind. But it had driven Cardinal Chingada, when it reached him, into a frenzy of bewilderment as he tried in vain to make out exactly, or even vaguely, what the Professor was up to.

> 'By a curious stroke of good fortune . . .' (wrote Mrs Trigger, laboriously and with many lickings of her pencil point) 'our later researches were signalized by the discovery of a second papyrus fragment of forty-two lines, all incomplete, written in third-century cursive and so providing us with a *terminus a quo* for the writing on the other side. This, which is an upright formal uncial of medium size, can be tentatively assigned to the middle or end of the second century, though Professor Harnack, with all his usual brilliant powers of analysis, has put forward the thesis that Fr. 2 consisted of extracts from the Gospel according to the Egyptians, an early Gnostic work covering apparently the same ground as the Synoptists and circulating principally in Lower Egypt where it was probably composed. The question is, however, complicated by the extremely divergent views. . . .'

Mrs Trigger sighed heavily and looked up from her work. She took a long, slow look around her and shifted uneasily in her

74

chair. Then she put down her pencil and stood up. Very slowly, almost as if in a kind of trance, she began to circle around the room turning her head this way and that as if trying to locate the source of some impression—a smell perhaps, or music faintly heard. Yet it was neither a smell nor a sound that she was searching for, trying to pin down; it was . . . it was. . . . She didn't know what it was. A feeling? Yes, a feeling. She had felt it before in this room. It seemed to be stronger with every visit. But it was a feeling so vague, so indefinable, so unlike anything she knew. . . .

In the furthest corner of the study stood the Professor's safe, a massive black Victorian contraption with a brass plaque bearing the royal arms on the front, and a handle cast in the form of a fist clutching a thunderbolt.

On her second circuit Mrs Trigger passed the safe and then stopped, retraced her steps and came to a standstill in front of it. The feeling was strongest here.

Her eyes riveted on the safe, she took a step towards it, then another until she was standing pressed against it, unable to advance and there was a dazed look in her eyes and her face began slowly to take on a look of surprise, then pleasure, a gradual dawning of bewildered ecstasy. Slowly at first she began to move her body against the hard black mass, up and down, up and down, then faster till her breath was coming in hard little gasps, and faster again, her mouth open now, her eyes closed tight, a tiny dribble of saliva at the corner of her mouth, faster . . . faster. . . .

# 6

'These scars now,' asked Father Singleton. 'On your knees, you say?'

Miss Thirkell looked down at her hands writhing like white animals in her lap. She was a shy person. Finding herself alone in Father MacCord's office with a strange man—even a priest—

was acutely distressing. And he asked such strange questions. . . .

'The result, perhaps, of former . . . austerities?' Singleton went on. He tried to keep his voice neutral but was unable quite to conceal his lively professional interest. 'Penances? Prostrations?'

'Yes, Father.'

Miss Thirkell's knees, together with the stigmata under discussion, were hidden by her skirt, a tent-like structure of black gaberdine, unfashionably voluminous. Miss Thirkell was no siren. On the contrary, she was neurotically modest.

'Hum! I see . . . I think you had better show me, don't you?'

Miss Thirkell hesitated, looked away.

'You need have no secrets from me my child. Look on me as your confessor. And remember I am here to help you.'

Blushing, Miss Thirkell raised her hem a cautious inch.

'Higher.'

Another inch.

'A leeetle higher.'

Father Singleton swallowed hard.

'My, those *are* scars.'

He turned away and Miss Thirkell lowered her skirt.

'Tell me,' said Singleton, staring out of the window, 'has young Heavenspur ever shown any . . . interest in these . . .'

He waved a hand in the air and let the sentence trail away.

'I'm afraid I don't quite know what you mean, Father.'

'I mean, has he ever . . . has he ever asked to look at them, for instance?'

'No, never.'

'Never . . . touched them?'

'Oh, no, Father.'

Hummm.'

Singleton began to sidle round the room until he stood behind Miss Thirkell's chair. From here he could observe unobserved. Those breasts . . . Wherever he stood they impinged on his vision, making it increasingly difficult to concentrate on what promised to be a delicate interview. They seemed to be alive under her thin blouse, struggling against their restraints like

76

huge silken eggs about to hatch something. Crocodiles? He cleared his throat.

'Does the name Flake mean anything to you?'

At the mention of the name Miss Thirkell jerked as if someone had hit her and blushed till her makeup ran.

'Ah, I see it does . . . Painful memories I'm afraid?'

'Oh, Father! It was terrible. He—'

'Of course, of course,' said Singleton in a soothing voice. 'Believe me, I have no wish to rake up old wounds. . . . But there is something I must ask you . . . Would you like to see him again?'

At this, sobs racked Miss Thirkell from top to bottom and she twisted about in her chair as if trying to escape from ropes which held there. Singleton had never seen anything like it. She *rippled.*

'I'd . . . rather . . . die . . .' she said at last in a choking voice.

'I see, I see. Then we'll say no more about it.'

Singleton leaned forward and patted her gently on the shoulder, saying, 'There.' Then he pulled his hand away sharply and put it behind his back. He took a step away from the chair.

'What is your name, child?'

'Rowena.'

'Well, now, Rowena, we can't let things go on like this, can we?'

'But I haven't *done* anything, Father.'

'Of course you haven't. I mean we can't let Heavenspur go on like this.'

'No . . . I suppose we can't. But . . .'

'Certainly we can't,' said Singleton a trifle sharply. 'What would happen to your good name, to the good name of the firm, if these licentious employees were allowed to rampage unchecked? What would your uncle the bishop say? No, Rowena, he must be brought to book, and smartly. And if we are going to make him see the error of his ways, which we are, then I must have your help.'

Miss Thirkell sounded a little uncertain: 'Of course, Father. I'll do whatever I can if you say so. But Mister Heavenspur is *dreadfully* persistent.'

All the more reason,' said Singleton, bug-eyed and perspiring all over his sallow face, 'why we should act at once.'

# 7

Father MacCord, speaking in his capacity as General Manager, claimed that the firm of Mulvaney and Toon, while it had always adhered to Traditional Values (i.e. cheap labour and wide profit margins) was nonetheless Moving With The Times.

The firm's claim to thrusting, with-it, New-Church modernity was based principally on its possession of its very own computer. This machine—a dilapidated second-hand Aleph-6 Watkins (series-B Vatican conversion)—was housed in a cramped apartment behind the Devotional Articles showroom, together with Mr Cranley Heavenspur, its operator.

It could be said that even the computer Adhered to Traditional Values, in so far as it accounted for a sizeable proportion of the firm's profits. When it was not being used for the mundane necessities of costing, stock-taking and the like, it was not allowed to lie idle. The surplus computer time (there was plenty of it) was sold at competitive rates to overworked clergy (also plentiful) for the purpose of saying requiem masses. The Watkins could reel off up to a hundred years of requiem masses in a matter of nanoseconds. 'Our prayer wheel,' MacCord would remark to interested clients with what he fancied to be an Impish Smile. Then, readjusting his face to simulate Transcendent Spirituality and casting his eyes up to the ceiling, 'This simple device has, I like to think, delivered more souls from Purgatory than a thousand generations of mere human intercession. Subject, of course, to a Higher Will than ours.' And sometimes he added, 'All in all, it's a godsend.'

Cranley had his own use for the computer. It was a godsend to him, too.

The morning of his interview with Father Singleton he sat

at the input desk setting up a programme. One hand banged at the punch keys. The other clasped a half-eaten Heavenspur Special—a sandwich of Cranley's own devising which contained a dangerous-looking mixture of bean sprouts, cottage cheese, tahini and water-melon-pickle, generously smeared with vindaloo paste. Cranley held that a Heavenspur Special was the nearest thing to a scientifically perfect meal that could be limited by two slices of bread.

'Cannon,' he muttered. 'Smooth bore . . . nine pounders . . . twenty-seven . . . hmm . . . Twelve pounders, rifled . . . eight . . . Fremont . . . twelve pounders . . . hmm . . .'

His teeth came together in mid-sandwich. Clamp! Squish!

In front of him, on a sort of elongated music-stand, three books lay open: Livermore's 'Numbers and Losses in the American Civil War', Henderson's 'Life of Stonewall Jackson' [Vol. 1], and Von Neumann and Morgenstern's 'Theory of Games and Economic Behaviour'. A small pile of other indispensable volumes—works by Schelling, Rapoport, Puhvogel, and Richardson's 'Statistics of Deadly Quarrels'—lay nearby under a basin of holy water. The presence of this last item is explained by Father MacCord's insistence that the computer be subjected to a thorough Aspersion before and after each run of masses. It was vital, he said, to preserve an element of Ritual in these acts of Intercession, which otherwise risked becoming purely mechanical. In practice, however, Cranley was extremely reluctant to do any aspersing as the only obvious result was to produce short-circuits in the machine.

The question of the aspersions was a frequent cause of friction between Cranley and his employer.

Clack . . . clack . . . clackety-clack . . . (munch) . . . clack.

Cranley paused and leaned forward to turn a page.

'Early . . . Where was Early? . . . Ah.'

Clack. Clackclack.

Ten minutes later he sat back satisfied. He allowed himself a short, pre-H-hour breather during which he finished his sandwich and licked his fingers thoroughly.

He tore off the tape, got up and crossed the room to the

computer input. He wound the tape carefully on to the spools. A green light came on.

'Fire!' shouted Cranley.

His finger stabbed down on the start button and the tape disappeared into the guts of the machine.

Cranley moved to the centre of the room and assumed a Napoleonic stance. The hum of the computer became in his head the rattle of musketry, the boom of cannon, the thunder of horses' hooves and the screams of eviscerated patriots. A wild light shone in his eye.

In thirty seconds it was all over. A red light came on, the din of battle cut out with a last loud click, and the printer began to chatter. Cranley unfroze and rushed to the output. With trembling hands he tore off the protruding end of the paper strip.

> BATTLE OF CROSS KEYS JUNE EIGHTH
> EIGHTEEN SIXTY TWO FREMONT MUST FLEE
> THE SCENE OR BE ANNIHILATED IN FIRST
> TEN MINUTES.

'Really?' said Cranley.

RIP, added the machine from force of habit.

A buzzer sounded from the office intercom on the wall. Mechanically, Cranley put out a hand and unhooked the receiver.

VOICE OF MISS THIRKELL: Mr Heavenspur?

CRANLEY: (*electrified*) No! Yes!

MISS T.: Oh, Mr Heavenspur . . . I wondered . . . I thought perhaps . . .

CRANLEY: Yes? Yes?

MISS T.: . . . you would like to . . . see me . . .

CRANLEY: (*fervent voice*) Soon!

MISS T.: I'll be, I'll be. . . . I'll be working late tonight . . . so we could . . .

CRANLEY: Where? Where?

MISS T.: (*audible blush*) The Statuary Stockroom, it's . . . quiet there.

CRANLEY: Indeed it is. WHEN?

MISS T.: Well . . .

CRANLEY: Seven? Six-thirty? SIX?

MISS T.: Six, if you like . . . (*big effort*) Cranley.

CRANLEY: Oh yes I do, Miss Thirkell, I do. Miss Thirkell, may I call you—

MISS T.: (*click*).

CRANLEY: Rowena, Miss Thirkell?

For a full minute Cranley stood where he was with the receiver clapped to his ear. He began to sway dangerously. An expression of vapid concupiscence draped itself across his face. Leaving the phone dangling from its flex he tottered to his chair and sat down. With his arms hanging rigidly by his sides and his legs straight out in front of him he looked like a man who has just fallen backwards from an aeroplane.

'She called me,' he muttered. 'SHE called ME.'

He shook his head three or four times.

'Oh, Miss Thirkell,' he said languishingly. 'OH, Miss Thirkell.'

He pulled himself together. His knees had gone into catatonic ataraxy and nothing could be done with them until he had given the back of each joint a number of sharp jabs with a pencil. Then he looked at his watch. Four o'clock. He felt a tide in the affairs of C. Heavenspur which was going to make the Great Wave of 1834 look like a local disturbance in Archimedes' bathtub. It was time to consider his strategy. He picked up Von Neumann and headed for the door.

# 8

Upstairs in the Manager's sanctum Father Singleton was doing some inter-office phoning of his own.

'Good,' he purred into the mouthpiece. 'Gooood. . . . Be brave now, Miss Thirkell. . . . Yes, I know. But remember, it's for his good as well as yours . . . You must trust me, my child. I shall be near to help if I am needed. Goodbye now.'

He put down the phone and rubbed his hands.

'It's on, James. The Statuary Stockroom at six.'

'You have prepared our, ah, positions?' asked MacCord.

Singleton raised an eyebrow. *'Our* positions?'

'You'll need a witness, I take it?'

'Thank you, James. That won't be necessary. No need for you to involve yourself in this unsavoury business.'

MacCord was visibly dashed.

'But I thought—'

Singleton raised a hand to cut him off.

'Not another word James. There is more at stake here than the efficiency of the firm. I surely don't have to remind you that it's my head will answer for this operation if anything goes wrong.'

'Surely, Singleton—'

'I appreciate your concern, James. But you have heard my last word and it is No. I mean to handle this unpleasant task myself.'

# 9

Cranley spent a profitable hour locked in a cubicle in the Buyers' Washroom with Von Neumann across his knees. Tactically, he felt, his position was not too strong. Since there was a numerical parity of forces, he would need a steady nerve and a cool head if he was going to surround and annihilate Miss Thirkell. Either he could stake all on a single onslaught in the hope of crushing her centre in the first minutes of the encounter; or, by playing on her natural sympathies, he could endeavour to wear her down until she had committed her reserves, and then try a paralysing flank attack on the Chancellorsville pattern. He spent several minutes in a careful analysis of the various possible pay-offs and then, with a rush of blood to the head, decided that even a disaster was worth the candle and the hell with strategy.

Morally fortified, he emerged from his cubicle and crossed to the line of washbasins. They were surmounted by a long strip of blotchy mirror. Its reflective powers had been severely diminished over the years by the onset of a shameful and disfiguring disease, probably a mutant form of potato blight.

He washed his face and hands in hot water. Then he washed his face in cold water to promote a healthy, glowing complexion. Then he washed his hands again in hot water as they had gotten cold in the preceding operation. Finally he combed his hair carefully, with the aid of the mirror.

He wiped the comb on the seat of his trousers and was just putting it back on the shelf where he had found it when the door of the Washroom opened. He turned abruptly, with a Guilty Start that any Dostoyevsky hero would have envied. He was not of Buyer rank and his presence in the Buyer's Washroom was a flagrant trespass.

'Oh!' said Cranley.

'Hullo!'

The newcomer looked to be some sort of Chinaman, probably not the heathen sort, as he was wearing a soutane and shovel hat. His teeth, Cranley noticed, were a strange colour, they had a sort of greyish glint to them. He stood in the doorway eyeing Cranley (narrowly) and making no move either to advance or retreat. Cranley for his part had no intention of vacating the washroom if it could be helped. His preparations were still incomplete. The intentions of the Chinaman were inscrutable.

In the end it was Cranley who broke the deadlock. He went to the door, took a firm grip on the Chinaman's elbow, and steered him out into the corridor.

'It's that way,' he said, pointing.

'Oho?' said the Chinaman, as if acknowledging a full-scale revelation. 'Thank you.'

'That way,' Cranley repeated.

He gave the elbow a tiny push in the direction indicated and the Chinaman obediently pottered away down the passage.

Cranley spent quarter of an hour practising facial expressions in the mirror. These expressions—Tender, Beseeching, Urgent, Cave Man No. 1, etc.—he had developed over a period of months from crude prototypes. They were specifically calculated to ravage Miss Thirkell's front-line defences and sow the seeds of confusion in her rear areas.

'I . . . love . . . you . . . Miss Thirkell,' mouthed Cranley, fixing the mottled looking-glass with a gaze of desolated longing.

When he left the washroom it was a quarter to six.

# 10

The Statuary Stockroom formed part of a complex of storage areas which occupied the basement and sub-basement of the shop premises. It constituted an infringement of the Second Commandment on a massive scale: dark, cavernous, and stuffed to the roof with a clutter of graven images of all sizes and shapes, made of every conceivable material from bakelite to cast concrete, and in styles ranging from Bavarian super-kitsch to Sutherland neo-rococo. The dominant themes were Crucifixion tableaux, likenesses of the Virgin, and Holy Family conversation pieces, but these were only leitmotivs in a luxuriant undergrowth of assorted saints, prophets, anchorites, angels, archangels, evangelists, martyrs and martyresses kneeling, praying, flying, expiring, recumbent in packing cases, rampant on pedestals, or attached by ropes, nails, chains or skewers to trees, crosses, racks, wheels, gridirons or large stones.

It may be noted in passing that, in addition to the more popular lines in hagio-mimesis, the firm kept a large stock of multi-purpose saints, aimed at the off-beat market. These Special Lines were the work of a group of artisans known as the Lay Brothers of the Oblates of St Remigius. The Brothers had the special knack of executing their works with a cunning and deliberate vagueness which was the outcome of generations of technical innovation and astute market research. Thanks to the Brothers, Mulvaney and Toon were able to supply, unhesitatingly and unblushingly, any saint whatever, regardless of whether they had ever heard of him or her before. This solved the stocking problem in a manner both elegant and economical, besides providing a neat example of *e pluribus unum* in reverse. Father MacCord had been heard to remark that between Saints Evurtius and Machutus there was, thank God, no great gulf fixed.

In the centre of this gloomy jungle of gesticulating totems stood Mr Cranley Heavenspur, biting his nails, like some furtive iconoclast, peering about him at the piles of crates, scanning the horizons of the shelves, scrutinising each dark recess. He looked at his watch. In the half light he had to hold it to his nose as if testing it for odour. He was a few minutes early. The shop would be closing now. At any moment she would be here. And then? And then (surely) she would. . . . And he would. . . . And together they would . . . and even . . . ! (secure from interruption).

Abruptly his heartbeat switched from four-four to six-eight and the palms of his hands began to tingle.

'Mr Heavenspur?'

Her voice was a tiny uncertain whisper, hardly louder than the swish of her skirt as she entered the room; the door closed behind her with a timid click. Yet these sounds beat on Cranley's burning ears with all the violence of sunrise on the Mandalay autobahn. His head whirled. His vision blurred. He stood rooted to the spot. And she glided towards him from the wrong end of a gigantic telescope, her blouse a smear of white against the blackness in which she swam.

A few feet from him she stopped and looked, not at Cranley, but around her, as though scrutinising the faces of a crowd of passers-by from under some lonely station clock. Then she turned to Cranley who hadn't moved.

'Mr Heavenspur?' she said again. 'Cranley?'

Cranley ignored her. He shook his head once, slowly, but his eyes were nailed to the poetry that was in motion beneath the scanty material of her blouse.

Miss Thirkell divined that her audience was captive but its attention needed redirecting. She seemed to gain a little confidence and her voice took on a peremptory edge.

'Mr Heavenspur!'

Cranley wrenched his eyes away, one at a time.

'Mr Heavenspur, why must you always look so . . .' (she searched for a word) 'intense?'

'Do I?' asked Cranley.

'I asked you to come here because I thought we might—' She stopped suddenly.

'Yes,' breathed Cranley. 'Oh, yes!'

'Yes what?' she asked, frowning.

'We might. We WILL!'

'Mr Heavenspur, Cranley, I don't think you realise that my position in the firm is being made, shall we say, uncomfortable by your . . .' She stopped again. She had lost him. Huge weights had dragged his gaze downwards ten or fifteen degrees in the plane of the ecliptic. She took a step backwards.

'I do,' said Cranley absently. 'By my what?'

'Attentions,' said Miss Thirkell.

'My attention,' murmured Cranley. Then after a moment: 'You have it. It is yours.'

'Thank you,' Miss Thirkell said. 'But that is just what I do not want.'

This time Cranley didn't even hear her. He only heard the Sirens singing and saw only the Scylla and Charybdis of Miss Thirkell's mammary equipment.

He let his breath out with a rush and advanced, bent on shipwreck.

Miss Thirkell took two more steps back, tripped, spun round, nearly fell. Then she was off. And, with flight giving rise to pursuit in the traditional manner, Cranley was after her.

Away went Miss Thirkell down gloomy aisles between heaped shelves, dodging and twisting with desperate resourcefulness among piles of crates, scrambling and skipping over mountains of woodshavings, and always, miraculously, one jump ahead of the grasping hands of her maddened admirer.

'It's all right!' he shouted. 'Wait! Wait for me!'

But Miss Thirkell waited for no man. The saints and martyrs, as she whizzed by them, watched from the aisles with mournful

attention, their dead arms raised in rigid gestures of encourage-
ment, supplication or disdain.

'Rowena!' panted Cranley, wasting breath. 'Come back! I
only want to—'

The erotic steeplechase went on.

At some point in his career he had picked up a massive candle
and now he held in front of him like a weapon as he hurled
himself across the undiminishing distance which separated him
from his target. And the white blur of Miss Thirkell's fleeing
blouse darted, beckoned, bounded, danced and floated before
him, always just beyond his reach.

'Where will this end?' wondered Miss Thirkell.

She risked a glance back and he nearly had her, but she
twisted away and flung herself sideways through a narrow gap
between two huge boxes. The boxes clawed at her as she passed,
tearing her clothes. If she could only widen her lead by as much
as a yard, it would enable her to get to the door and give her the
time to get it open. But where was the door, which way? Down
here?

She turned a corner and stopped dead, flinging out her arms.
She had taken a blind alley and was trapped. She turned, panting, at bay. Tigerish, Heavenspur was nearly on her, only feet
away, triumph in his face, galloping down between the boxes
like Libido on a racehorse. A weapon! She would fight. She
grabbed for the first thing that came to hand. It was a hand. She
pulled. It was attached, unsurprisingly, to an arm. She pulled
harder—and like an avalanche of petrified swallow-divers a
teetering mountain of Holy Mothers Of God rained headlong to
the floor in front of her. Plaster cracked and shattered, wood
splintered, limbs cracked like a forest of matches, heads flew
like cannonballs, and there, prone among the debris as if
engulfed in some dreadful massacre—Father Singleton, a
crucifix in one hand and a portable tape-recorder in the other.

Miss Thirkell fainted. Father Singleton scrambled upright and
shook himself to arrange his strangely disordered clothing.

'Heavenspur!' he thundered. 'You have gone too far. Only
one way is left for you . . .' He raised one arm—that holding

the tape recorder. '. . . and that is OUT!'

'But I only wanted—'

'For ever!' said Singleton, standing immobile like a vengeful signpost.

'. . . to measure,' said Cranley, waving his candle vaguely towards the unconscious Miss Thirkell. And quite suddenly he began to cry.

Miss Thirkell, making her way home over Vauxhall Bridge, stopped and looked down at the water. It looked cold and dirty. She decided to do nothing irrevocable, at least until the weather got warmer.

The next morning orders came for Father Singleton to hand over to MacCord and return to Rome. Paper Bag Phase two was under way.

MacCord and Seamus drove Singleton to the airport.

# II

The day's work over, Comrade Secretary Chang donned his decadent-western-bourgeois-imperialist outfit, set his bowler at a not-too-jaunty angle, and slipped out of the Embassy. He used the front door in order to avoid the cloud of CIA men who hung around the back entrance disguised as milkmen, meter-readers, hopeless alcoholics, window-cleaners, boy scouts, dirty-picture salesmen and limbless war veterans.

Chang's umbrella tap-tapped happily down the Edgware Road and along Praed Street.

Chang's daily, or rather nightly, visits to an unobtrusive two-room flat in Bayswater were an open secret at the Embassy. Indeed, in the rather specialised atmosphere of the Embassy, any other kind of secret was rare. It was known that Chang paid the rent on the flat out of his own pocket, and therefore it was generally assumed that Chang was keeping a mistress. The more that Chang denied that this was so, the more his comrade colleagues winked and knew he was lying. So Chang persisted in his denials, knowing that if it became known that he actually didn't have a mistress, the fat would be in the fire. If his shameful secret ever got out, if Comrade Peng, for example, ever found out what Chang was really up to in his Bayswater *garconnière*, then Chang could say goodbye to everything that made life worth living.

*The Secret*: Chang's mistress had a twenty-four-inch screen, simulated walnut cabinet, Living Colour on four channels, comprehensive remote control attachments and both inside and outside aerials. The Comrade Secretary was a television addict.

Despite this little weakness, Chang was a good Comrade.

As he let himself in at the front door and began to climb the stairs, he whistled snatches from 'The East Is Red'.

# 12

When the expected ransom failed to materialise, it became depressingly clear to Porson's captors that they had arrested the wrong man. A mood of disgust and disillusion settled on the Famaka constabulary.

A meeting was held in the Police Post to decide on future action. All three constables attended. The Sergeant with the miraculously-adhering fez presided.

'We must decide what to do with him,' said the Sergeant. 'The situation is becoming intolerable.'

'Intolerable,' the constables agreed. 'We must do something.'

'He cannot stay here for ever,' said one.

'By God you are right, Kassim,' said another. 'Ours is a small prison.'

'And not a hotel,' said the Sergeant.

'By God, it is not,' agreed the constables.

'He makes much noise,' said Kassim.

The constables agreed that this was so. Indeed it was so. Even through the thick walls of his cell Porson's screams were clearly audible twenty-four hours a day.

'If we shot him,' said one of the constables, 'he would be less of a burden to us.'

'We cannot shoot him, Mouchtar,' said the third constable.

'He has no tribe,' said the Sergeant. 'Certainly we may shoot him.'

'To shoot a holy man, would that not be a great sin?'

'I never heard,' said Kassim, 'that among the Nazrinis there are holy men.'

'The hand of God has touched him. Has he not vision? Have we not seen with our eyes how he tears at his clothes.'

'By God you are right, Sallal,' said the Sergeant, struck by the justice of this observation.

'By God he is,' said Kassim and Mouchtar. 'We have seen it.'

'How then can we shoot him?' asked Sallal.

'Indeed we cannot.'

'Then we must free him.'

'By God, Sallal,' said the Sergeant. 'That is what we must do.'

From the cells the screams were getting louder. Porson was having another of his visions—beetles, millions of them.

# 13

'Goodnight,' said the Announcer, and vanished.

'Goodnight,' responded Chang politely, and stayed put.

The image of a clock was replaced by a buzzing snowstorm of random electrons. Chang picked up the remote control mechanism and ran rapidly through the other channels. Everywhere it was the same story—random electrons.

He was a creature of habit and one of his habits was to make quite sure that every station had finally and definitely closed down before he himself did so.

He sighed and switched off. It was always a bit of a wrench when another evening's Total Viewing came to an end. He hung the control set carefully on the hook screwed into the side of his chair. Then he leaned back and stared at the ceiling.

Total Viewing was a phrase Chang had coined to describe his approach to the TV experience. It implied, among other things, Total Absorption, Total Dedication, and Total Suspension of the Critical Faculties. To these ends Chang had organised his environment with a single-mindedness that bordered on the psychotic. In order that no time should be wasted away from the set, every foreseeable need had to met *in situ*. The result was Chang's Viewing Chair, a chair so ingenious, so complete, so loaded with technology—pendant, inset, obtruding and circumpatent—as to resemble the nightmare creation of a gadget-maddened dentist. Without moving from his seat Chang could not only exercise absolute control over the four TV channels, but he could also make tea, prepare light meals, switch on or off every light in the flat, dictate letters, telephone (in case of accidents he had the number of every late-night repair service in the Greater London area), regulate the room temperature, draw the curtains and open or close the front door. There were also controls for adjusting the length, concavity, viewing axis, and angle of incidence to the floor of the Chair itself.

Right now Chang was doing none of these things. He was staring at the ceiling and thinking.

There was a worried look on his face—a bad sign.

It was a source of embarrassment to Chang that he had never quite achieved that relaxed rigidity of countenance which reveals nothing whatever of its owner's underlying emotions and mental processes. He knew, of course, that the West demands one hundred percent Inscrutability of its Orientals, but try as he might his face was always just a fraction too scrutable to qualify. However, Chang reasoned that if the ideal—No Information—was unattainable, his best strategy was to settle for second best—False Information. In place of the utter blandness which persistently evaded him he had worked out a series of facial expressions calculated to mystify and mislead the enemy as much and as often as possible.

*The expressions:*

1. When he was happy, he smiled. There was nothing he could do about it. Besides, it was adequately misleading: few

Europeans, he found, were willing to take his face at its face value. The idea that a smiling Chinaman might conceal nothing more devious than a happy Chinaman was too much for their simple minds.

2. When thoughtful he managed to look tolerably Bland.

3. When he was worried, he managed to look no more than Thoughtful.

4. When, therefore, he looked Worried, it meant that he was something worse than worried—a regular tempest in the psyche. Right now, for instance, it meant that he was Scared Stiff.

He had been that way, on and off, for several days—ever since, in fact, the day he had had The Thought.

On that day he had, as usual, left the Embassy at five o'clock as happy as a Marxist-Leninist sandboy, without a care in the world beyond a ticklish choice of channels that would have to be made at around nine-thirty. Then, half-way through an episode of 'The Man From CRUNCH' (a hair-raising serialisation of the life of a police dog-handler), it had happened. The Thought hit him with the violence and abruptness of a heavy-calibre machine-gun bullet, assassinating his innocent tranquillity and turning his tripes upside-down in the space reserved for them.

The concept which had brought this havoc on Chang's mental well-being was, at the moment of its epiphany, more of an intuition than a consciously-formulated idea. Verbalisation came later, and with it came full realisation of just how nasty a spot he might be in.

*The Thought*: If Secretary Peng is sending back confidential reports on me (which I suspect he is) and if those reports are going to who I think they are going to (which I think they may well be) and if the recipient of those putative reports is identical with the recipient of my confidential reports on Comrade Peng namely Comrade Colonel Wou Chang Chen (which is a reasonable assumption and anyhow follows from my second premise) then it is not unreasonable to assume that unless the new secretary due on the first of the month is a cunning and devious fiction wrought and put about by Comrade Peng to cause alarm and despondency (especially mine) then the new secretary may not as Comrade Peng asserts be the replacement of him (Peng) BUT MINE!

Such was the master-product of Chang's deductive faculties —a fine example of just what can be done with a good diplomatic training.

Its implications, if true, were clear enough—*no more television*.

# 14

Cranley left the Museum when the Reading Room closed and hurried across the playground towards the bus stop. It was already dark and there was a cold wind blowing. He put his head down against it and retracted his neck into the upturned collar of his black leather trenchcoat.

He waited twenty minutes for a 159 bus. Finally four came, all empty. Cranley got on the last one, knowing it would annoy the conductor. He went upstairs and made his way to a front seat, foiling every attempt of the driver to overthrow him by sudden random changes of speed. He sat down and put his briefcase on the seat beside him. His eye fell on an evening paper lying abandoned at his feet. He picked it up. An item on the front page caught his eye.

FLAKE MYSTERY DEEPENS. STATEMENT SOON?
DOCUMENT COULD BE 'TIME-BOMB' SAY EXPERTS.

The mysterious silence surrounding the eminent Oxford historian and statistician Professor J. G. Flake since his return from Africa five days ago after an unexplained absence of nearly two years is deepening. Our reporters have been unable to gain admission to the Professor's remote Berkshire hideout where, according to a source close to the Professor, he 'seems to be doing a lot of resting'. Meanwhile controversy continues to rage over the mystery document Prof. Flake is reported to have brought back with him. If, as some experts confidently predict, the document in question really is the fabulous 'Q-Text', the consequences could be earth-shaking, involving, according to one eminent authority, 'a complete revolution in our thinking about the basic tenets of the Christian faith'. Rumours that the Archbishop of Canterbury is to convene a special— (Cont. back page Col. 1).

Cranley read this much, giving it only half his attention. He understood nothing of it. He was mildly interested that the Professor seemed to have become involved in some kind of scrape with the press. Flake had been Cranley's tutor at Oxford for a time, and Cranley remembered him with a certain affection, even admiration. But on his way to the back page he ran into a report on a new rocket launcher that was being used in Vietnam and the 'Flake mystery' slipped from his mind. Besides, he had problems enough of his own.

He put a shilling into the conductor's hand and got a ticket which he rolled up and put behind his ear.

He got off the bus at Piccadilly Circus.

He pushed his way through the rush-hour crowds with little sense of direction or purpose. Some nervous mechanism must have registered a need for food and he soon found himself in a restaurant—one of those all-plastic eateries tricked out in a style best described as Fish-Finger Baroque. Cranley ordered something and ate it. His mind was elsewhere. When he had finished, he pushed away the plate and rolled a cigarette.

It was three days since he had parted company with Mulvaney and Toon. Since the débâcle he had spent most of his time in the Reading Room of the Imperial War Museum collecting background material for one of his minor projects. During this period what had started out as a feeling of vague unease had grown to a leaden pumpkin of despair. Denied access to the firm's computer, his chances of finishing his monograph in time to meet the deadline set by the 'Journal of the Society for Army Historical Research' were nil. Publication had been promised, his reputation as good as made. His 'Alternative Optimal Strategies in Jackson's Shenandoah Valley Campaigns 1861-2' would have launched him triumphantly into a great career. And then he could have said goodbye for ever to the loathéd precincts of Mulvaney and Toon. Now, at the eleventh hour, victory had slipped from his fingers, as it had, indeed, from those of many a general before him. Prospects were bleak. Where was he going to lay his hands on the kind of money he would need to buy computer time? Two hundred pounds an hour was the going rate for anything about the capacity of desk calculator and his present resources wouldn't buy five minutes on a steam-driven abacus.

On the subject of Miss Thirkell Cranley was curiously numb. Feeling might or might not return to the traumatised areas, but for the moment the catastrophic outcome of what might so easily have been a beautiful relationship played no part in his current conflicts. Even if—

Plonk!

A sharp slap on the table announced the arrival of his bill, prone under a large, red, red-nailed hand. Around the edges of this hand the corners of the bill stuck out desperately. 'Needs help', thought Cranley. The hand continued to lie where it had fallen, pinning the bill to the table. Cranley's eyes moved up along the arm which connected the hand to a large, red-haired waitress.

The waitress hooked Cranley's eyes with a hard and meaningful look and then redirected his gaze to the imprisoned bill. Then she lifted her hand.

Obediently, Cranley picked up the bill. It said FOLLOW ME in the Beverages, etc. column.

The waitress was already moving away towards a tangle of plastic lianas which masked the entrance to the kitchens. Cranley followed at his best speed, skating in her wake over the half-inch slime of putrescent organic detritus which filmed the kitchen floor. She held open the door. Cranley passed through. The waitress closed the door and returned to her duties. Cranley was left drinking in the pure night air in an alley which C. Dickens would certainly have labelled Noisome. His immediate environment consisted largely of tall metal bins, some of which were marked SWILL, some REFUSE and some GARBAGE. This system of nomenclature interested Cranley. He had not known that the phylogeny of rubbish was so sophisticated. He started opening a lid here and there in the hope of learning more about the distinguishing features of the different categories. As he warmed to his work, he bent a gratified thought to the waitress who had so kindly introduced him to this taxonomist's paradise.

He was stooping with a lighted match over the contents of his third or fourth bin when he felt himself roughly seized from behind, his arms pinioned, and a cloth bag drawn over his head.

Cranley was carried, squealing and kicking, to a car that was standing at the entrance to the alley with its engine running. He felt himself bundled into the back seat; doors slammed and the car moved off into the traffic. Cranley continued to protest in a muffled manner through his bag until, getting no response, he ceased. They drove around for a long time. Cranley resolved to answer no questions and to reveal no information whatever. This made the silence in the car total, as so far no one had asked him anything. Perhaps this was why they were so quiet—they were trying to think up some really difficult questions?

Finally a voice broke the silence: 'This is a one-way street, you stupid idiot.'

'Janie Mac!' exclaimed a second voice, presumably the driver's, in a thick Irish accent.

Cranley had been wondering whether his captors might be police officers on some sort of a spree or exercise. He had begun a search of his memory banks for any felonies or misdemeanours in his past history which might lend a retributive flavour to his present situation. Parking tickets, for instance, or Overdue library books? He now abandoned this line of reasoning, having recognised the voice of the first speaker: Father MacCord's.

MacCord now spoke again. 'I expect you're wondering why we've brought you here, Heavenspur?'

'Where?' asked Cranley, truculently.

'Chiswick,' said the stupid idiot's voice.

'Another word out of you, Seamus,' snarled MacCord, 'and I'll slap a penance on you will keep you busy till you start drawing your pension.' And to Cranley he said, more smoothly: 'You'll find out, my dear fellow. Soon enough.'

'If it's about those aspersions—'

'It is not.'

'Miss Thirkell, then?'

'Indirectly,' admitted MacCord.

'Then I wish to—'

MacCord cut him off. 'Patience, Heavenspur. Patience.'

The car stopped. Someone helped Cranley out. He heard the doors slam and the car driving away. He felt a guiding hand on his elbow and MacCord's voice in his ear.

'This way.'

MacCord led Cranley through the gate, across the tiny front garden and round the side of the house to the back door.

'Here we are,' Cranley heard him say. And he added, for some reason, 'More or less.'

'What do you mean more or less?' asked Cranley, enemy of sloppy speech-habits.

'Roughly,' said MacCord as he knuckled out a longish message in morse on the panels of the door. 'Approximately. That kind of thing.'

Footsteps were heard on the other side.

'Isaiah twenty-four seven,' muttered a hoarse voice, within.

'Revelations six twenty-two,' sang out MacCord.

Jackpot. There was a prolonged series of unlocking noises. The door opened and Cranley was steered over the threshold. He heard some whispering and the hoarse voice saying, 'Upstairs.'

Upstairs Cranley was unveiled. He found himself alone with Father MacCord in a small, brightly-lit, white-painted room with a bare wooden floor and a single, heavily curtained window. There was no furniture other than a pair of straight-backed chairs, and a table cluttered with electronic gear which Cranley did not recognise as a high-powered ultra-short-wave transceiver assembly.

'Sit down, Heavenspur, sit down,' said MacCord.

Cranley sat down and looked about him. MacCord began to

pace about with his hands clasped behind his back. In his tweed suit he looked like a man waiting impatiently for opening day on the grouse moors. Cranley ignored him. He studied a poster over the mantelpiece which read in Gothic capitals—

SET A WATCH O GOD OVER THE DOORS
OF MY LIPS

and, lower down in plain letters—

PROFANE TALK COSTS
LIVES

'How would you like,' MacCord asked as he began his third circuit, 'your job back?'

Cranley's heart missed a beat then hurried to catch up.

'You mean . . . ? You don't mean . . . ?'

'Oh I do, Heavenspur, I, ah, assure you.'

'You brought me here to ask me this? Why?'

'Because I want to *know*,' said MacCord with great emphasis.

'Yes. But all this.' (Gesture.) 'I have a telephone.'

'And I have a telephone,' MacCord assured him. 'In fact, several.' He had his beads out now and was tossing them backwards and forwards over his forefinger. He kept up his pacing. His route took him round and round Cranley's chair which stood in the centre of the room. His method was to cover three sides of a square with his eyes on the floor and to look at Cranley only when passing directly in front of him. On Cranley this intermittent, almost stroboscopic contact with his interlocutor was beginning to have a dizzying effect. 'Unfortunately,' MacCord went on, 'in matters of, ah, procedure, my hands are tied. There are conventions, codes. In our work there is inevitably an element of cloak and, ah, dagger. Childish, perhaps. But necessary.'

'Very well,' said Cranley. 'What about my job now?'

'First a question. You know Professor Flake?'

'Vaguely,' said Cranley vaguely. 'What has that got to do with this?'

'Oh nothing, nothing at all. . . . You were on, ah, good terms?'

'I suppose so.'

Father MacCord covered a few yards in silence. Then—

'Look here, Heavenspur. If, and I say, ah, if, I was to do you a little favour . . . I need hardly say that I have the ear of the, ah, Directors . . . Or should I say ears?'

'Ears,' said Cranley.

'Thank you. The point is, would you in return be prepared to do . . . A proof of good faith if you like . . . Nothing difficult, a little, ah, job merely . . . for us?'

'Who is us?'

'Who is us? Who is us?' muttered MacCord, evidently subjecting the questing to a thorough analysis. 'Us,' he said finally, 'is . . .' he lowered his voice to a respectful whisper, 'the Church.'

'The Church?'

'Militant,' said MacCord.

'So,' said Cranley, 'I do something for you—'

'For us,' said MacCord. 'For us.'

'For us. And you do something for me.'

'The very thing!' beamed MacCord. 'In a nutshell.'

'The ears of the directors?'

'*And*, I need hardly add, an increase, a substantial increase in your, ah, emolument.'

Cranley thought hard.

'Well,' he said at last. 'What is it?'

'Ah!' said MacCord. 'Well now. That . . . hmm.'

Without warning MacCord stopped dead in his tracks, staring fixedly ahead of him. His view was drastically circumscribed by the fact that he was standing in a corner of the room. Then he seemed to come to a decision. He whirled to face Cranley, his eyes flashing like neon signs.

'Heavenspur,' he hissed, emoting heavily, 'Mother Church is in mortal danger! You—' he thrust a melodramatic finger almost into Cranley's left nostril '—have been chosen to enter the lists in her defence against the forces that beset her.'

'I see,' said Cranley, a trifle taken aback by the turn things were taking. 'Where are these lists located and what do I have to do?'

# 15

Downstairs in the kitchen MacCord addressed the hoarse-voiced man:

'He's all yours,' he said. 'Begin when you like.'

'Training is it?' said the hoarse-voiced man licking a large spoon which he then replaced in a jar of peanut butter.

'Yes,' said MacCord. 'The usual. But it's a rush job.'

'How long have we got?'

MacCord was buttoning up his coat.

'I want him ready for an operation in three days.'

'Snot much,' said the hoarse-voiced man, doubtful.

'Three days,' said MacCord with his hand on the door. 'No later. Time is running out.'

MacCord went out through the back door.

The hoarse-voiced man took some things from a cupboard and laid them on a tray.

He went upstairs.

He found Cranley, still sitting on his chair, rolling a cigarette. He put down his tray on the table.

'So you're the new man.'

'Heavenspur,' said Cranley. 'Where's Father MacCord.'

'Felix,' said the hoarse-voiced man. 'Gone. It's you and me now. You interested in poetry?'

'No,' said Cranley.

'Concrete poetry?'

'No,' said Cranley.

'Pity,' said Felix. 'You might have heard of me.'

'Felix?' said Cranley. 'No.'

'Oh,' said Felix. Abandoning any further attempts to find a

common ground, he turned away and began to fiddle with the things on the tray. Cranley watched him. He saw a man of about forty wearing tennis shoes and a roll-neck sweater with leather patches at the elbows. He looked like a torpedo standing on its tail. He was very thin, he had no shoulders, and his neck ran straight up the sides of a head which was bald on top and somewhat pointed. It only needed a fuse and you could have sunk the *Lusitania* with him.

'It's outside my field,' Cranley said, sugaring the pill.

'What is your field?' asked Felix absently. He was inserting the business end of a gigantic hypodermic into an ampoule the size of a baby's feeding bottle.

'Probability,' said Cranley. *'What's that?'*

Felix turned with the needle at the 'present'.

'Just a little pick-me-up,' he said. 'Roll up your sleeve.'

Cranley took off his overcoat.

'Is this really necessary?' he asked.

'Oh, vital.'

Cranley took off his jacket and rolled up his sleeve, very slowly.

'What? What?'

'Methedrine,' Felix explained. 'We've a lot to get through.'

Cranley's eyes boggled as Felix advanced. The syringe loomed at him bigger than a bicycle pump.

'Just hold still,' Felix said.

'OWWWW,' Cranley said.

'There,' Felix said. 'Nothing to yell about.'

He helped Cranley into his jacket and stood back to await developments. Cranley sat slumped in his chair for a minute or more. Then his face slowly took on a look of the most profound astonishment. He sat up straight. Then he smiled a broad smile of pure delight and began to look about him like Adam on the First Morning.

'Migod!' he exclaimed. 'This an interesting place you've got here and no mistake.'

'I'll say,' said Felix. He opened a drawer in the table and took out a clipboard with a pile of flimsy typewritten sheets. 'This is a standard training manual,' he said. And added for his own benefit, 'I think.' He tore off the top sheet and handed it to Cranley. 'This is your schedule. Memorise it and then destroy it.'

Cranley took the paper and studied it with passion.

'There's an awful lot,' he said. 'When do I sleep?'

'I know,' said Felix. 'You don't.'

'Fascinating,' murmured Cranley, still reading. 'Most of it seems to be in Latin.'

'It's all in Latin,' Felix told him. 'Security precaution. If this stuff got into the wrong hands it could be dynamite.'

'Amazing,' said Cranley, devouring the text. 'Fantastic.'

'You understand it then?' asked Felix on a note of surprise.

'Not a word.'

'Ah,' said Felix. 'It's just as well. The less you know the better. In case you're interrogated.'

'I see. What you're trying to say is that innocence defined in terms of ignorance is a sufficient defence against evil despite evidence to the contrary from any number of works I could cite ranging from the book of Genesis to the works of William Golding despite wide differences in fundamental outlook?'

'That's about the size of it,' Felix admitted. 'Here. Give me that.'

He snatched the sheet from Cranley's hand and applied a match to one corner. Cranley's hand and arm remained in the position they had been while he still held the paper.

'Well in that case,' Cranley continued disputatiously, 'just how do you explain the position adopted by the French existentialists?' He broke off. His attention had been caught by the flaming paper. 'I hadn't finished,' he said reproachfully.

'Doesn't matter.' Felix stamped out the last glowing fragments on the floor. 'We've got to get started. Now . . .' His voice came through a bit muffled as he began to suck a burnt finger. 'Have you ever been tortured?'

'No, I don't think so,' answered Cranley. 'Not properly.'

'Well it can't be helped. We'll come back to it later if we have time. . . . What about you see?'

Cranley waited. 'You see what?' he asked finally.

'Unarmed Combat,' Felix said a mite tetchily.

'O.I.C.,' said Cranley. 'You mean—'

'I mean,' Felix hissed savagely, baring his teeth, 'KILLING WITH THE HANDS.'

'Never tried it,' admitted Cranley.

'Well try it now.'

'On you?'

'On me.'

Cranley stood up slowly and shifted uneasily on his feet. He felt like a bad actor not knowing what to do with his hands. He cleared his throat.

'Just like that?'

'Come on!' roared Felix. 'KILL ME!'

Cranley frowned, took a hesitant step forward.

'Yah!' jeered Felix. 'Sissy! What are you ULP!'

His breath came out with a whoosh as Cranley hit him just above the belt with a fist from which the knuckle of the second finger protruded wickedly. Felix folded like a railway signal dropping and as his head went past, Cranley hit him again on the back of the neck with the edges of both clasped hands.

Felix sank slowly to his knees, his mouth open, his face blank, his arms locked to his sides. Then, an inch at a time, he bent forward from the waist until his chin rested on the floor.

'Good lord,' said Cranley, observing these reactions with amazement.

Felix lay rigid at his feet like an inverted square-root sign, supported by his chin at one end and his toes and knees at the other. His backside rose in the air, high and motionless, and on this Cranley, leaning forward, tapped politely, as being the portion of Felix nearest to hand.

'Felix. I say, Felix.'

No answer. Cranley tapped again, harder. Anxiety began to get the better of his embarrassment and he renewed his apostrophes with increasing urgency.

'Felix! Felix! Say something!'

Felix remained without sound or motion. Cranley lay down

on the floor next to him and with his head to one side tried to peer into Felix's face. 'Are you dead, Felix?' To catch any response, however feeble, he cupped a hand behind the ear which was not pressed to the boards. Felix's face had turned a dirty grey.

'Are you?' Cranley insisted.

'No,' said the murdered man in a barely audible whisper. He opened one eye and then the other. 'No, I don't think so.'

Cranley scrambled up and began helping Felix to his feet. Felix reassumed an upright position by painful stages. Finally he was more or less vertical again, but subdued, very subdued. Cranley was brushing off his teacher's clothes with outbursts of apology and commiseration. Felix raised a slow hand for silence.

'Where!' he wheezed in a much diluted voice. 'How?'

'A freak of fate,' babbled Cranley. 'You are the victim of an accident. I had no idea this would happen, none. It was something I happened to read in a book.'

'I should have guessed,' said Felix sadly.

'Of course if I'd realised . . . I know how silly it sounds.'

'He read it in a book,' said Felix, addressing a point in space about eight inches in front of his nose. 'Can it be that I'm getting too old for this sort of thing?'

He shook his head several times with the greatest care and then turned again to Cranley.

'How much do you know about disguises?' he inquired in a mournful voice.

*Part Three*

# NOBIS QUOQUE MILITANDUM

# I

From his underground headquarters Cardinal Polenta held sway over an empire of frayed nerves and repressed uncertainties.

Signs of disintegrating morale were beginning to manifest themselves: Menschmeyer could no longer remember whether or not he had infiltrated the John Birch Society; Fegato was trying vainly to hide his anxiety behind a fixed smile that each day looked more like a plastic banana; and Balai-Rose, shaken to the core by repeated blows to Procedural Routine, had taken to walking about shrugging and muttering to anyone who would listen, 'It's all so *diffuse.*' Even Polenta was badly shaken by the discovery that twenty-seven suspected Aphthartodocetists had been omitted from the List owing to an error in filing.

And of course the increasing tempo of work on the Cardinal's various projects meant a proportional increase in strain for Singleton, the Cardinal's leg-man. Daily he sweated more copiously, daily his blue chin grew bluer and his sallow face sallower as he padded, stalked, pattered or sidled—according to his mood and the exigencies of the moment—from room to room, department to department, along corridors, tunnels, ramps, passages, hallways, stairs and galleries in a hopeless attempt to co-ordinate and oversee the jungle of concurrent and conflicting activities that mushroomed on all sides.

The task was too much for him; in the last analysis it could not be otherwise. For, like the rest of them, Singleton lacked the one thing without which their world was only shadows, reflections in a distorting mirror which, however accurately observed, were ultimately devoid of meaning. Neither Singleton, nor anyone else, shared the Final Secret. The key which would unlock the hidden Purpose of their work was not vouchsafed them. That knowledge was Polenta's and his alone.

It was natural enough that Polenta should guard it jealously. A man who intends to impeach the Pope as a heretic and schismatic would be a fool to cry his intentions from the housetops. At least, not until he is good and ready.

And Polenta wasn't ready yet. Not quite.

Meanwhile, in the rest of the Holy See, already humming with preparations for the Great Council, ripples were felt. Nothing definite, nothing palpable—no more than a premonition of something in the air, something strange and perhaps a little menacing. It was a tiny backwash only of Polenta's vast expenditure of covert energy. But it was enough to cause a shaking of heads in the Congregation of the Holy Office, an exchange of furtive whispers in the Apostolic Chancery and the inditing of nuanced memoranda in the Secretariat of State.

Two people in the Vatican were left untouched by the miasmas of worry and suspense that were creeping over the landscape. One was H.H. and the other was Cardinal Nuvoletto.

# 2

'Just how long ago was he was took funny, as you put it?'

Mrs Trigger hesitated before answering.

'I don't really like to say, Doctor. It's been coming on for a few days now. He's been getting, well . . . weaker like.' For some reason she blushed. 'And this morning when I come up with his tea same as I do every morning and a bit of bread and cheese just like he enjoys, he doesn't like toast you know, burnt bread he calls it, well, there he was like you see him now.'

'I see,' said Doctor Blakiston thoughtfully. 'Well, well, well. Just a bug, I expect. There's been a lot of it about. That'll be all I think, Mrs T. I won't keep you from your work ha ha.'

'You'll ring if you need anything, sir.'

She went out. The Doctor's eyes followed her through the door. There was something about her . . . something . . . He couldn't put a name to it. The way she had brushed against him as she turned to go. An accident? If she had been twenty years younger he might almost have said . . . No, it was ridiculous. He shrugged it off and turned to his patient.

The Professor lay on his bed staring up at the ceiling. He was giving as good an imitation of a corpse as a man could give without actually being dead: shrunken, doll-like appearance, staring eyes, half-open mouth, waxy skin.

Doctor Blakiston set about making some elementary tests, firing off the occasional bedside-manner inanity as he worked.

'Well now. Feeling a bit under the weather, are we?' For example.

The Professor said nothing, just lay motionless with his gaze fixed on the plaster above his head.

'Nothing to worry about, you know. Mustn't mope. Mustn't let it get you down. Worst thing you could do. But we'll have you back in harness in a brace of shakes. Hm?'

(Breathing regular but slow and shallow. Pulse sluggish, 33 to the minute. Pupils dilated. Temperature 97·4. Reflexes, none.)

'Hum! Not hibernating, are you?'

No answer.

'Had our bowels open today, have we?' he asked gaily, shining his little torch down his patient's throat.

Nothing there. Tongue looks a bit gluey though. He shone the flashlight into the Professor's ear and made a wry face. Filthy. He opened the pyjama jacket and did a little stethoscoping. Heartbeat a little weak, perhaps, but regular enough. Then some knuckle-tapping. No congestion. Must be something rare. Sickle-cell anaemia? Mudd's disease? Hope it's nothing catching.

'Any vomiting?' he asked.

No answer.

109

'Any pain?'

No answer.

'Let's have a look at the old tummy then.'

He peeled back the bedclothes and opened the Professor's pyjamas. His eyes bugged at what he saw. So that's it.

'Good lord,' he said to himself. 'Most extraordinary. Who'd have thought he had it in him?'

He prodded around a bit just for the form and then replaced the bedclothes hurriedly.

'Right as rain in no time at all. Just you lie there and take it easy,' he pronounced as he packed up his kit.

On his way out he stopped in the hall for a word with Mrs Trigger. 'A good rest,' he said. 'That's all he needs. Keep him warm, plenty to drink, and an aspirin every four hours. Nothing to worry about. If he gets any worse, call me.'

'I do hope he's going to be all right, sir. If anything . . . happened, like, well, I don't know what I'd do.' Unaccountably she blushed again.

'Mrs Trigger,' said Doctor Blakiston seriously, 'has he had any, well, friends here lately?'

'Oh no, sir. He won't see anyone.'

'And he doesn't go out much?'

'Not at all, sir. Not since he come back that is.'

'So he doesn't really see anyone?'

'Excepting me of course, sir.'

'Quite so,' said the Doctor thoughtfully and left.

When he got back to his surgery after his morning rounds, he spent half an hour buried in Kleinscheidt's 'General Pathology'. Then he picked up the telephone.

The phone bell rang in another surgery on the other side of town.

'Murdoch speaking . . . Ah, hello Blakiston. . . . What's that? . . . No! Hypogonadism? . . . Hyperaesthesia? . . . Good lord! . . . Shrunken, you say . . . Like a brussels sprout . . . Overdoing it? I'll say! Listen, old boy, it's funny you should ask. I had a case of my own the other day. . . . Yes, identical . . . Krapp's syndrome, or I'm a Dutchman. Coincidence, eh? . . . Yes. No bigger than a mushroom stalk. . . . No a little one, button mushroom . . . Hmm. . . . Fellow named Hawkins. Local man. . . . Prescribe? I didn't have time to prescribe a damn thing, old boy. Blighter died the same day. . . . Yes, out like a light . . . The cook! You must be joking. . . . Yes! Listen Blakiston, what about a joint effort for the B.M.J. on this? Could be the making of us. . . . Good, good, good . . . Well, keep in touch, won't you? . . . Yes. . . . Yes. . . . Right. So long, old boy.'

When Doctor Blakiston put the phone down he rubbed his hands eagerly.

In his surgery on the other side of town Doctor Murdoch rubbed his.

# 3

For anyone who lives, as Comrade Secretary Chang lived, in a society dedicated to permanent revolution, survival is a constant preoccupation, especially for the ambitious. Yet it is curious that such a state of affairs does not necessarily put a premium on personal initiative. Chang, for example, had found that self-effacement is the best protection. It makes for slow promotion but in the long run it is worth a wardrobe-ful of bullet-proof waistcoats.

His decision to steal the 'Q-document' can, therefore, only be interpreted as an act of desperation stimulated by the imminence of a perceived threat—the threat in this case being the replacement, return to Pekin and possible disgrace of Chang, engineered by Comrade Peng with or without the connivance of Comrade Colonel Wou Chang Chen. It was the cornered rat syndrome, in a word.

Not that Chang felt like a cornered rat: he felt better than he had felt at any time since he first became aware of the executioner's axe hanging poised over his Viewing Schedules. His plans were laid. He was ready. The march he was going to steal on Comrade Peng would make the Long March of 1934 look like a stroll in the Vienna Woods.

He stood before his mirror, considering his image. He smiled so that his teeth gleamed dully in the harsh light. These classy gnashers, of hand-tooled stainless steel, seemed to Chang to be an almost perfect blend of modern materials and traditional craftsmanship. He had bought them on the black market when he had been stationed in Yunnan in 1949. They had cost him half a year's salary but they were simple and economical to maintain and were still as good as new. He flashed them again experimentally in the mirror. They certainly added a touch of distinction. Then a frown appeared on his face. Perhaps they added just a touch too much distinction. Perhaps they were even . . . a dead giveaway? But if, in the interests of preserving his anonymity, he discarded his teeth for the duration of the operation, would he not be losing more than he gained? It was essential to his plan to pass unnoticed wherever he went, and to this end his disguise was fashioned. But which was the least noticeable—a priest with stainless steel teeth or a priest with no teeth at all? He slipped them out and weighed them in his palm. Then he turned again to the mirror and confronted himself suspiciously. He put on a trial smile. The effect was horrible, he had to admit it. But he had made up his mind. He would just have to avoid smiling.

He wiped off the teeth on a piece of Kleenex and placed them in their red plastic travelling-case. He placed the case among the socks in his drawer. He gave a last twitch to his dog collar, which had a tendency to entrench itself in his double chin. He fitted the shovel hat to his head. A final squint in the mirror. Splendid. He grinned and shut his mouth hastily. Must watch that.

He picked up his black briefcase and left the flat.

The street was comparatively quiet. It was the slack-water time between the end of the rush hour and the beginning of the last complete performance.

It was only a few minutes' walk to the station but Chang took a roundabout route in order to throw off, or at least fatigue, anyone who might be following him. He proceeded, at first, furtively, with many a sidelong glance from under the brim of his hat. But the world at large seemed as indifferent to the presence of the Reverend Father Chang in its midst as it had been to that of Comrade Chang the Diplomatic Attaché.

About half an hour later he entered Paddington Station by the back way and bought a second class return ticket to Pangbourne. Needless to say Pangbourne was not his real destination. To cover his tracks further he proceeded to tour the station buttonholing railway officials and pestering them with lengthy and complex enquiries about trains as far apart as Harwich and Holyhead.

Finally, to crown these cunning manoeuvres, when his train was already waiting at Platform Five, Chang went and stood around ostentatiously on Platform Six, where no train was waiting. He stayed there until a general clashing of doors and a chorus of whistles and hoarse shouts from Platform Five brought him flying across the intervening space in a last-minute sprint which brought gasps of admiration from a jaded group of stationary porters posed around a trolley-load of dripping fish-boxes.

Legs whirling and soutane flapping Chang wrestled open the first available door of the already moving train, flung his brief-case aboard and himself after and flopped down in a seat panting.

The compartment had one other occupant, a man of about thirty with close-cropped hair and wearing a brown corduroy suit which looked as though it had been slept in for several years, real clochard's pyjamas. He sat in the window seat opposite Chang and though their knees were almost touching he seemed completely unaware of Chang's presence. He was staring straight ahead of him with eyes that boggled glassily; a fixed frown of permanent surprise wrinkled his forehead. As soon as Chang realised that the stranger was staring through, not at him, he relaxed a little, complimenting himself once again on the impregnable anonymity of his disguise. He assumed the rather rigid expression of his travelling-companion to be part and parcel of British train etiquette. He had never experienced it before but he had been briefed on that kind of thing. Anxious not to be outdone, he composed his own features into a mask of intense indifference and averted his head a little so that he could, while appearing to be engrossed in the passing vista of terraced slum-buildings, keep the stranger under observation by watching his reflection in the grimy window-glass. Chang had the uncomfortable feeling he had seen him somewhere before. But it was difficult to be sure. With the exception of a few favourite television personalities all Caucasians looked alike to him.

Half an hour went by. The lights of the city were left behind. The tableau in the compartment remained static. Chang suffered in silence. The stranger remained equally silent except for an occasional loud grinding sound from his teeth. Chang could see the muscles in his jaw working spasmodically but had no way of knowing if he was actually suffering, or to what extent.

Chang wondered how long this silence could last. He had no intention of being the first to take the plunge. He had something ready, of course, if called on to speak, a remark about the weather. He was going to say, 'Lovely day isn't it, old boy?' But he wasn't going to speak first if it killed him. He practised his sentence under his breath. He rather liked the sound of it. Chatty, informal, but giving nothing away.

Time passed.

They were well into the open country now. Unrelieved darkness pressed against the glass an inch from Chang's nose. He had a crick in his neck which was fast developing into a full-scale cramp of the sternoclidomastoid. But still he didn't move and he didn't speak. He bore it and remembered not to grin. What had started as a point of British Etiquette was becoming a point of Socialist Honour. . . . 'Lovely day, isn't it?' Chang kept running his sentence over in his head, trying little variations of phrasing and intonation. The pain grew worse.

There came a point when Chang could stand it no longer. He wrenched his head round and picked up the briefcase which was lying beside him on the seat. It was held shut by a complicated snarl of buckles, flaps, snaps, straps and hasps designed to make it difficult to open. After a great deal of fumbling he managed to get a hand in and groped around inside for the copy of the 'Catholic Herald' which he had put there before setting out, thinking to give a finishing touch to the externals of his persona. A great deal of planning had gone into this operation. His hand felt the edge of the newspaper. He grasped it firmly and gave a sharp pull. A heavy nine millimetre parabellum pistol fitted with a screw-on silencer shot from the bowels of the briefcase and landed with a thump on the foot of the man sitting opposite.

Chang gave a yelp of mortified surprise and threw himself forward to scoop the weapon from the floor. Horror-stricken, he began feverishly to stuff it back into the case and refasten the relevant buckles, flaps, snaps, etc.

The stranger, meanwhile, subjected to the raw kinetic energy of fifty-seven ounces of nickel steel landing squarely on his toe, was electrified to the extent that he moved his right foot two inches nearer his left and, speaking almost inaudibly between locked jaws, muttered, 'I'm sorry.'

Chang, as soon as he had got the case shut, shrank back in his corner sweating and shaking and glancing wildly in every direction except his front. He raised his newspaper in front of him in a desperate attempt to erect some kind of barrier between himself and the consequences of his blunder and tried in vain to restore his shattered calm. A whole drama of failure and humiliation was rising to life in his imagination—the stranger reaching politely but inexorably for the communication cord, the hurried arrival of official feet, the interrogations, torture perhaps, fruitless denials, the inevitable unmasking, deportation, scandal, disgrace. General Wou had a way with blunderers; the best Chang could hope for at his hands would be ten years digging latrines in Mongolia, and, at the worst . . . what? The firing squad? The Black Tanks? The Reducers? There were a million ways to die, and all of them nasty. It was cruel. It was unjust. Chang had a sudden movement of revolt against the wickedness of his fate. To be robbed of his prize at the eleventh hour, to be frustrated in the very act of bringing off a coup which might have brought him in a single bound to the top of his profession and made him the darling of his chiefs, the envy of his peers and the cynosure of his inferiors—it was more than a man could take. And he, Chang, would not take it. He would fight. He was cornered but not beaten. Let this stupid Englishman do his worst.

Arming himself with an appropriate thought of Chairman Mao—to wit: THE THOROUGHGOING MATERIALIST DOES NOT KNOW THE MEANING OF FEAR—Comrade Chang fired his first shot.

'WELL?' he yelled defiantly from behind his newspaper.

And, realising that the 'Catholic Herald' had served its purpose now that the thing was out in the open and the time for skulking in his trenches was past, he flung it to the floor with a gesture that fell only an inch or two short of the Heroic and glared full in the face of his antagonist.

The stranger responded to these stimuli by (i) subtly altering the focus of his eyes so that he now looked *at* Chang rather than through him; (ii) adding another wrinkle to his frown.

'Well what?' he asked.

'Well!' shouted Chang. 'IT'S A LOVELY DAY ISN'T IT?'

The stranger considered this proposition.

'Well . . .' he began and then stopped.

He looked out of the window. Then at his watch. His frown became a look of intense introspection. He ground his teeth slowly, meditatively and loudly, sending shivers down Chang's spine.

'To tell the truth,' said the stranger finally, 'I hadn't noticed. Until you mentioned it, that is.'

He bent an apologetic look on Chang, whose mouth had fallen open into a toothless gape. The stranger interpreted this reaction as being due to some shortcoming in his response to Chang's remarks. He decided to add a few words of explanation.

'I've been rather busy. Studying and so forth. Crowded schedule. Very little time.'

He nodded to himself several times and began to grind his teeth again.

Chang, lost in contemplation of the threat that was no threat, suddenly realised that his mouth was open and shut it with a snap. The stranger jumped. There was a pause during which Chang carried out a quick Revision of Ideals and the stranger continued what seemed to be an all-out campaign to reduce his molars to bleeding stumps.

Chang modulated his voice to convey Easy Cameraderie tinged with Clerical Paternalism and holding his hand casually across the lower part of his face he said: 'My name's Smith. Father Smith.'

'My name,' said the stranger, 'is . . .'

'Yes? Yes?'

'I'm afraid I can't tell you.'

'You've forgotten?'

'No. Not exactly.

'Then,' said Chang, leaning forward, 'it's a Secret?'

'Well,' said the stranger, 'a bit of both really. I'm travelling incognito, you understand, for, er, business reasons.' And he added with a touch of wry remorse: 'They told me my name of course, that is my . . . well, my business name. But there was so much to remember.'

He sighed.

'So you've forgotten the Secret?' said Chang, plainly disappointed.

'Exactly.' (Nod, grind.) 'Very tight schedule.'

'I understand perfectly,' said Chang. 'The same thing happened to me myself. Frequently. Would it be offensive to enquire your destination?'

'Ah, there you have me,' said the stranger.

'Another Secret?'

Chang was beginning to enjoy himself.

'Oh, no,' the stranger said.

He dug in an inside pocket and produced his ticket. He read it carefully, starting with the fare, place of origin, serial number, destination, date and class, then turning to the back for a brief résumé of Conditions of Issue and a few relevant observations regarding the bye-laws to which, in the Company's opinion, the Bearer was subject.

He put the ticket back in his pocket and looked up. Chang was eyeing him expectantly.

'Pangbourne,' the stranger said.

'Pangbourne,' exclaimed Chang. 'What a coincidence! I'm bound to go there myself.'

He might have enlarged further on the delightfulness of the situation, in fact he intended to, but the stranger put a sudden end to the conversation by standing up and pulling down a briefcase from the rack behind him. He took out a book and a notebook, replaced the case on the rack and sat down. He began reading the book and making notes in the notebook. Chang, peering covertly across, saw columns of figures with marginal annotations. Advanced algebra of some kind? Or a code perhaps?

'I see you're interested in mathematics,' he said cunningly.

'No,' said the stranger, scribbling busily away without looking up.

'Part of your studies then? A boring but necessary feature of the curriculum? I understand how well.'

The stranger looked up with sudden interest. 'You do?'

'Oh yes.'

'In that case, I'd very much appreciate your advice on this bit.'

He shoved the book across to Chang and tapped with his pencil to indicate the focus of interest.

'Whatever may be the philosophical interpretation of Bernouilli's formula, the mean of $x$ when weighted by $T_x$ is KP. If we wish to know whether L differs significantly from KP we must add up the terms of $T_x$ so as to find the probability that L differs from KP by more than it actually does, and in the same sense, remembering that the variance X of KP is $KP(1-P)$, but fortunately a sufficient approximation can be obtained from the Poisson limit where KP is fixed as $K \rightarrow \infty$.'

'Ticklish,' said Chang. 'Tricky.' He gave a short laugh. 'I'd have to use my abacus for that one.'

'That's it of course,' said the stranger, suddenly gloomy. 'No abacus. Exactly my trouble. We're in the same boat then.'

Chang felt sufficiently confident to air an idiom.

118

'Without a paddle,' he agreed.

The stranger continued to stare at his book but it was evident that he was no longer reading. He had put his pencil in his mouth. Gradually the glassy, bewildered look returned to his face. Chang waited to see what the results would be on the pencil when the tooth-grinding started up again.

Matters were at this pass when the train made, as it had taken to doing quite frequently, a jerky stop at a very small station. Outside in the yellow gloom of the platform a voice moved up and down the train calling threateningly, 'Pangbourne. Pangbourne.'

'Here we are then,' said Chang and looked across expectantly. But the stranger had relapsed into total immobility. The pencil stuck out sadly from his mouth like a forgotten thermometer.

'Pangbourne,' said Chang. 'Your stop I believe.'

'Ah,' said the stranger, not even looking at him. 'Well, goodbye.'

'Goodbye,' answered Chang.

Nobody moved. Chang stared at the stranger. The stranger stared out of the window. Chang knew what was coming—an impasse. He picked up his briefcase and started putting his newspaper away, making as much noise as possible in the process. Then he shut the case, again with a maximum of fuss. He looked at the stranger. Nothing. He stood up. He looked again. Nothing.

'You've changed your mind,' said Chang reproachfully.

'Yes,' said the stranger absently, not looking round.

'Well *I* have to go,' said Chang and waited.

Nothing.

'Well goodbye,' said Chang.

'Goodbye,' said the stranger.

Chang stepped out on to the platform. The door slammed behind him with unnecessary violence.

When Chang had gone, the stranger took an envelope from his pocket. His movements were slow, as if each movement had to be planned in advance and separately executed.

The envelope was marked:

TRAVEL ORDERS—PART TWO.
OPEN ON REACHING PANGBOURNE.
DESTROY IF CAPTURED.

He took the pencil from his mouth and used it to slit open the envelope. There was a single sheet of paper inside with an address on it. He read it carefully.

Chang spent the remainder of the journey locked in the second-class lavatory. The smell was revolting.

# 4

The train disappeared into the night at the other end of the platform. Cranley found himself alone in the yellow fog dispensed by a couple of regulation-pattern paraffin lamps.

The only other passenger to descend from the train had already disappeared about his business.

Cranley looked slowly about him. There was a bench under one of the lamps. He walked over and sat on it. He took out the envelope marked INSTRUCTIONS PART TWO and opened it. There was a typewritten slip and a map. The map showed him how to get to the Professor's house. The instructions told him to proceed thither 'furtively'. On arrival he was, among other things, to eat the map. Getting there was going to be the problem. The map, for security reasons, hid as much as it revealed. It showed a maze of intersecting lines representing country roads and in the centre a nexus of some sort, presumably the village in which he was presently located. There was a profusion of arrows, dotted lines, compass bearings, and a few references (in Latin) to prominent landmarks. All place names, road numbers and so forth had been studiously omitted. Cranley studied the map conscientiously for a good ten minutes, turning it this way and that. Then he gave up.

It began to rain.

The station, on closer inspection, turned out to be even more unsavoury than it had seemed at first sight. In daylight it might have had a sort of derelict charm, but at night it resembled nothing so much as a ramshackle set for a low-budget remake of 'The Ghost Train'. Cranley felt his respect for the Professor increasing. If the station was in any degree a microcosm of the locality as a whole, then for Flake to immure himself in such a place argued the dedication of an old-style anchorite. Cranley had a sudden picture of the Professor, vastly bearded, perched in an oak tree round which clustered admiring rustics with baskets of country produce which the Professor, muttering, would draw up on a rope. It played hell with the legs, too, pillar-sitting. Cranley remembered the story of St Simeon carefully replacing the maggots that had tumbled from his festering thigh with the admonition: There, eat what God has provided for you.

Yes, Cranley thought, I have certainly underrated him.

He ran the Station Master to earth in what, judging by the smell, was a combination latrine and ticket-office. He was sitting with his feet up on the pot-bellied stove, reading a tattered copy of 'Spicy Pics'. He had a big nose covered with minute blue veins and big black pores. His responses to Cranley's questions were on the laconic side. Cranley classed him as Surly-Unhelpful. The Station Master classed Cranley as a Serious Hindrance to the Unmolested Pursuit of his Functions.

'Excuse me.'

The Station Master removed his finger from his right nostril and gave him a long stare of Official Disapproval.

'Yes?'

'Are there any buses?'

'Where you going then?'

Cranley waved an arm vaguely.

'I suppose you think this is Piccadilly Bloody Circus,' said the Station Master.

'So there aren't?'

'Right. They only run in the summer, don't they.'

'A taxi then.'

'Broke down last week, didn't it.'

He returned to his reading. Pause.

'I don't suppose,' said Cranley.

The Station Master looked up angrily.

'Are you still here? Don't you bloody know what time it is?'

Cranley looked at his watch.

'Eleven thirty-two.'

'Right. Midnight. So.'

'What about a bicycle then?'

'You're too late, mate. I just lent my bicycle to the other gentleman, didn't I.' There was a note of triumph in his voice.

In fact he was lying. He had *hired* his bicycle to the other gentleman at a figure which any impartial observer, even taking into account the local scarcity-value of wheeled vehicles, would have thought exorbitant.

'So there's nothing for it then?'

The Station Master had returned his nose to his paper and now gave a sniff which may or may not have been an affirmative.

'City types,' he said.

Cranley hesitated for a moment, wondering whether or not to go over and kick the Station Master in the groin. Instead he took a deep breath and put all the power of his lungs into a tremendous parting shot.

'GOOD NIGHT!' he screamed.

He turned and dashed from the room to the accompaniment of a voice inside his head saying: 'He stalked out, slamming the door behind him on the rueful functionary . . .'

Treacherously, the door did not slam. It was slightly too big for its frame and closed with a slow scrape and a polite thump. Station Master scores five points, courtesy of slipshod carpentry.

Cranley receded into the night mumbling with rage. The Station Master, filled with a blissful consciousness of a job well done, turned a page of his 'Spicy Pics', selected a finger, and began to explore his other nostril.

# 5

No moon. No stars. Not a house in sight. Not a car on the road.

The wind was rising, peppering Cranley's face with icy buckshot. He pushed his hands deeper into his pockets and hugged his coat round him.

His admiration for the Professor continued to grow. What a place to live. He adjusted his earlier picture of the Professor as dendrite to something more on the lines of Han Shan on Cold Mountain, and began to people the surrounding landscape (actually invisible) with misty bamboo groves, crags, cataracts, twisted woodcutters, a giant panda or two, the echo of mad laughter in a rocky gorge. . . .

A horse whickered from behind a hedge nearby. Cranley whirled towards it, startled. Mentally he stole the animal and thundered off into the night.

He sighed, shivered, and trudged on.

# 6

Mrs Trigger sat in the kitchen eating a lonely supper of toasted cheese and trying to make up her mind. At least, she told herself she was trying to make up her mind. In fact the battle had already been fought and lost, hours ago, days ago. The capitulation was made and admitting it was just a formality, ratification of a shameful pact already signed.

She chewed slowly. She was not really capable of doing two things at once—eating, and struggling with her conscience (or the few rags of it that remained). The cheese, cooling, grew rubbery and she chewed even slower. By the time her plate was empty, her mind was made up.

She washed the dishes and put them away. For a few

moments she stood in the middle of the room smoothing her apron with her big red hands and looking about her with half-focused eyes.

Then she left the kitchen and went upstairs and when she came down again she had a bunch of keys in her hand and her hand was shaking.

He employer, her victim, worn out, crumpled and discarded, lay in his bed staring as before at the ceiling. His catalepsy anaesthetised him against the stab in the back he had just received. For it was his keys, lifted furtively from his hard-wearing grey tweed trousers, that the treacherous domestic had just borne away.

Outside the study Mrs Trigger paused. Even here she could feel it. It had been growing stronger lately, spreading, a miasma of sensuality creeping through the house.

As she put her hand on the doorknob, the front doorbell rang.

She spun round, blushing, and for a moment she hesitated, fixed to the spot. Then, thrusting the keys deep out of sight in a pocket of her voluminous white apron, she crossed to the front door and hauled it open.

There was no one there.

She took a step outside and peered into the rainy blackness. 'Who's there?' she called.

No one, it seemed. She went back inside and closed the door.

To make quite sure, she waited a few moments with her hand on the latch, then suddenly whipped the door open and sprang out on to the porch. If there had been anyone there, she would have flattened him. But there wasn't. She closed the door again, went to the telephone in the hall, lifted the receiver and listened. Nothing. She went into the kitchen and tried the back door.

Again nothing. Ears playing tricks, then. She returned to the study and once more she paused outside the door, letting the first electric stirrings of pleasure brush her senses.

When she opened the door, a blast of pure excitement went through her like gamma radiation through a keg of butter. Her heartbeat doubled, her knees went weak, her vision blurred till all she could see was the safe, squatting in its corner and staring across at her like a great black eye. Hypnotised, she advanced towards it, fell on her knees in front of it. Breathing heavily, mouth half open, tongue protruding between her coarse lips, she began fumbling with the keys, feverishly trying one after another in the great brass lock.

It goes without saying that she was far too preoccupied to notice a pair of black shoes poking out from under the heavy curtains which masked the french windows. These shoes were the property of Comrade Chang, who was standing in them asking himself what the hell was going on.

Whatever it was, he was reasonably confident that he could turn it to his own advantage. Not for a moment did it occur to him that anything could go seriously wrong with the scene as he planned to play it.

The plan in question leaned heavily in its inspiration on the tactics employed by Jack the Duke, the titled amateur cat-burglar whose televised adventures enjoyed Chang's undivided attention every Wednesday evening between the peak viewing hours of 8.45 and 9.30. The Duke's uncanny competence and hundred-percent success-rate made him an obvious target for Chang's emulation. In addition there was a verve, an element of devil-may-care gusto, about the Duke's approach to breaking-and-entering which struck a responsive chord in Chang's romantic but fettered soul. Who but Jack the Duke, having (single-handed) knocked over the Bank of Ruritania in Lombard Street—ostensibly for a wager, but in reality for mere love of what he referred to as 'the game'—would have handed the entire proceeds to charity the next day?

Chang's admiration for Jack the Duke was at all times unbounded; in the present circumstances he was so far under the spell of his hero that he had to a large extent surrendered control of his personality and become a mere spectator of his own actions. It was not Chang who had arrived at Flake's house on a borrowed push-bike. It was Jack the Duke in a high-powered sports car, registration JD 1, watched from the side-lines by an admiring Chang. And, on arrival, it was the Duke, not Chang, who had carefully reconnoitred the gaff, noted the french windows as representing an easy point of entry (his cloth, he felt, debarred him from any fancy work on the drainpipes) and then, employing a ruse that was almost a trademark, rung the front doorbell to create a diversion, dodged round to the windows, forced them with a heavy screwdriver (read: microminiaturised oxyacetylene cutting tool) and found himself home and dry in the Professor's study.

He had not, it is true, given a great deal of thought to what he would do once he had penetrated the target area. Such details could normally be left to the Duke's natural cunning, split-second opportunism and phenomenal good luck. Chang had not, therefore, been unduly put out when, moments after his furtive irruption into the study, he had been forced to seek sanctuary behind the curtains by the arrival of a second party. Such things were only to be expected. It did bother him a little, though, that he could see nothing of what was going on. He had no means, even, of knowing who or what was doing all the panting, clinking, scratching, snuffling and gasping in the far corner of the room. He knew well enough what the Duke would do in case of such an uncertainty: he would choose the precise moment when the other occupant or occupants of the room had their backs turned to peep through the curtains for a quick survey of the tactical situation. The problem, of course, was to choose your moment.

In the event, Chang's decision was made for him.

Mrs Trigger, after going through the whole bunch twice, found the right key on the third time round. She held her breath, turned the handle, and pulled. The door swung open with a drawn-out squeak and Mrs Trigger abandoned herself utterly to the wave of concentrated pleasure which washed over her. She let her breath out in a long ecstatic moan, threw herself backward on the carpet, her back arched like a bow, knees drawn up, and plunged her hand under her skirt.

From this position she got her first sight of Chang's shoes sticking out under the curtain, separated from her bulging eyeballs by a few feet of blurred carpet.

She got to her feet and crossed to the window.

This rather bald statement hardly gives an accurate picture of the event, for the speed at which it was accomplished made it unique in the annals of physical science. The rapidity with which she transferred herself from Position A (on her back in front of the safe) to Position B (on her feet in front of the curtains) can only be explained on the assumption that the change was effected without passing through the space between the two points.

Her next move was to tear apart the curtains.

This revealed—not Jack the Duke, a sardonic smile hovering about his lips, his eyes glinting like twin chips of blue diamond —nor a startled, toothless, slack-jawed Chinaman in black soutane and shovel hat clutching a battered briefcase—but simply, a MAN. And if there was one thing Mrs Trigger needed at that particular moment in her life, that was it, a man. The answer to a maiden's prayer.

There could be little doubt what was going to happen next. The threat to Chang's physical and moral well-being was of the most obvious and immediate kind. The predatory intentions of the middle-aged maenad poised over him were beyond concealment. Lust, in a pure and concentrated form, was writ large on every portion of her large anatomy. It flashed from her eyes, it steamed in her hot breath, it oozed from her pores, it emanated in great waves from her vibrating carcass. Chang's Chinese goose was as good as cooked. And cooked it would have been had not Doctor Blakiston, on a late-night call, chosen that moment—the little moment of stillness before the breaking of the storm—to lean imperiously on the doorbell.

Mrs Trigger jerked her head round at the noise, her mouth twisted into the snarl of a lion disturbed at dinner. Then she turned again to Chang. Too late. Her hesitation had given Chang the extra second he needed to act in preservation of all he held most sacred. With a piercing yell and a crash of splintered glass he hurled himself backwards through the french windows and headed for the tall timber by way of the rose garden. Mrs Trigger, baulked but not beaten, was hardly less quick off the mark. A second later, with an answering yell, she was away in pursuit.

Doctor Blakiston, hearing the crash of the breaking window and the subsequent halloos, dashed round the side of the house in time to see what might have been a mangy black panther with a hysterical white elephant on its tail flash across the rainswept lawn and disappear into the night.

Without thinking twice about it, he gave some halloos of his own and set off at a brisk lope towards the spot where the fleeing pair had vanished.

When, ten minutes later, Cranley arrived on the scene, worn out and cursing, it was to find himself master of the deserted battleground. Open safe and all.

# 7

Cranley fell asleep in the train. At Paddington two porters extracted him and half-carried him to a taxi. He woke up for long enough to mumble an address at the driver. The cab set off with the driver shaking his head sympathetically.

'Fair brings you down, them trains, don't they?' he said over his shoulder.

Cranley didn't answer. He had fallen asleep again, curled up on the seat.

When the cab stopped outside his house, Cranley had to be helped out and set upright on the pavement. He had a parcel of some kind under his arm, wrapped up in what looked like a curtain. He took out a handful of money and held it towards the driver; his eyes meanwhile wandered uncomprehendingly over the world around him. The driver helped himself to the fare, plus a tip.

'I've taken a shilling.'

Cranley didn't seem to hear

'You all right then, are you?'

Cranley still didn't answer. He stood as if planted, one arm hugging his parcel, the other still outstretched in an eleemosynary gesture. The driver looked first at Cranley, then at the money in Cranley's hand. He took another shilling.

'I've taken another shilling.'

No answer. The driver got back in his cab and drove off aggressively. Cranley made a slow about-turn. He studied the terrain. He pointed himself towards a nearby tobacconist's.

'Morning, Mr Heavenspur. Been working late, then?'

'Ah,' said Cranley.

'Ounce of Boar's Head is it?'

'And a packet of papers.'

'Green?'

'Ah.'

'Beautiful day.'

'I believe it is,' said Cranley.

As he came out of the shop he imagined a cup of tea and stopped to buy some milk from a mechanical cow which stood handy. The machine took his sixpence and failed to deliver. Cranley kicked it till his foot hurt, then limped away.

He went painfully up the stairs to his flat and opened the door. He put down the parcel and picked up the telephone.

'I've got it,' he said wearily. 'No. I didn't see anybody . . . It was in a safe. . . . The door was open. I just took it. . . . I don't know . . . No. You come here. I'm going to bed.'

He took a pillow from his bed, turned on the gas fire, put the pillow on the floor in front of the fire, took off his coat, lay down with his head on the pillow, pulled the coat over him, and shut his eyes.

# 8

The sign on the door which previously had said:

BRIEFING ROOM

now said:

DEBRIEFING ROOM

This emendation was the work of Felix.

Behind the door in question C. Heavenspur, masterspy, had but recently spent three days and three nights learning his trade. And here shortly he was due back to give an account of his stewardship.

Felix, brush in hand, took a step backwards to let a critical eye rove over his handiwork. The sign, though lovingly wrought, yet displayed a fatal fault which could not long remain hid from an aesthetic faculty so refined and a perception so discerning. The original legend (simple black capitals on a plain white ground) had been neatly centred on the board in a manner which ensured the rhythmic balance and harmonic tension of the composition as a whole. This arrangement could hardly be bettered. And the addition of a two-letter prefix, far from bettering, had wrecked it. The layout now had a nasty list to port which it would be difficult or impossible to pass off on the public as a daring experiment in dynamic distortion.

'Tsk, tsk,' said Felix, shaking his head.

A little paint slopped over on to his shoe from the paint pot dangling in his hand.

Two possible ways of restoring the situation suggested themselves. He might remove the notice from the door—a five-minute job if a screwdriver could be found—and then, with a saw (tenon saw if available) remove the unwanted inches from the right-hand side of the sign, subsequently replacing the whole caboodle, suitably re-aligned, on the door. Or, alternatively, he could take the less drastic course of filling the offending space with a number of flourishes or whorls. The latter course would require some fancy brushwork, but one either is an artist or . . . not. No half measures.

'Brio is all,' murmured Felix to himself.

Then he fell into a deep brooding, wondering if it really was all.

He weighed the alternatives in his mind, this way and that dividing the swift cortical hemispheres. He pictured the re-emended sign thus:

And thus:

### DEBRIEFING ROOM

Both plans had their merits. It was not a decision to be made in haste, so he padded away down to the kitchen for some cold rice pudding and a good hard think.

# 9

The Great British Public got its first inkling of the night's events via the midday editions of the evening papers. Certain vital facts were necessarily missing, others obscured in the welter of supposition whereby the papers presented their ignorance of what had actually occurred in the guise of a sensational mystery. But in the stories under the headlines (FLAKE RESIDENCE NIGHT RAID DRAMA PUZZLE SHOCK, e.g.) lay imbedded a certain amount of hard information. The disappearance of the 'mystery document' had been discovered by a storm-troop of cycle-borne constabulary summoned by 'man of the hour Doctor Hamish Blakiston, close personal friend and trusted family physician' of the Professor. The Professor himself, it seemed, was unable to throw any light on the matter; he was at present 'in a coma' and 'doing well' in a local hospital. Mrs Trigger 'frenzied with grief' was under sedation in the same establishment.

Under a sub-heading MAN HELD it was revealed that a man found loitering suspiciously in the area was helping the police in their enquiries. He had been identified as Frederick Porson, journalist, of no fixed address. His behaviour was described as 'incoherent'.

Among the dramatic revelations not made public may be noted:

1. The hasty despatch from Washington of half a dozen CIA

men equipped with suitcases full of gold sovereigns and orders to find out what the hell was going on and buy a piece of the action.

2. The receipt by Cardinal Chingada of a message informing him that Paper Bag Phase Four was concluded and what next? He received this communication, for some reason, two hours *before* a message outlining the collapse of the Trigger-Hawkins network occasioned by the death of Hawkins and mysterious silence (defection? detection?) of Mrs T.

No mention was made in any quarter, public or private, of the state of mind of Comrade Secretary Chang. This may be summed up as: lamentable. How could it have been otherwise? Every time he asked himself what Jack the Duke would do next, he got the same answer: Jack the Duke could hardly be expected to extract himself from the hole Chang was in, if only on the grounds that it would be unthinkable for the Duke to find himself in a hole of that size and shape in the first place.

Furthermore, Chang had just learned that 'Comrade Peng's' replacement was due the day after next. Worse, Comrade Colonel Wou Chang Chen 'happened' to be due on the same day for a Routine Inspection.

Chang had a shower at his flat, changed into his working clothes, reinstated his teeth, and felt a little better. Then he sat down in front of the blank TV screen and recited some favourite morale-boosting aphorisms of Chairman Mao:

If your feet are made of clay, don't stand in the river.

Water runs downhill.

Only a man with a big mouth can eat a water-melon in one bite.

Etc.

A great comfort in times of stress. At the end of twenty minutes Chang was so far fortified by the homely wisdom of the Father of the People that he formed a Tentative Resolution:

'I will pull up my socks at all costs.'

# 10

Cranley's arrival at 24 Willow Crescent might have made medical history if there had been a medical historian, or even a second-rate ambulance chaser from the 'Lancet', handy to witness the event.

A long black estate car came to the gate and sounded its horn three times, a trinity of hoots. The gate was opened. The car turned into the short drive and drew up at the front door. Out of it stepped Seamus and Highpockets, both in their working clothes. They walked round to the back of the car, opened it and drew out an object five feet ten inches long weighing 154 pounds (11 stone).

Identity of object: C. Heavenspur, masterspy. Its condition: rigid, locked. Stiff as a board.

Highpockets turned to shut the boot and left Seamus holding Cranley's feet, while the remainder of Cranley's weight was taken by the back of Cranley's head, this being the only part of him in contact with t. firma. Meanwhile a third figure, Father MacCord's, wearing a racy deerstalker and reversible gaberdine raincoat, had emerged from the car. He carried a metal box some eighteen inches long by eight inches square. This was chained to his wrist by a businesslike chain broadly similar to those used for attaching elephants to teak logs, and vice versa.

When Highpockets turned back to resume his end of the burden, he gave a cry of surprise, as follows:

'Migod!'

And added by way of explanation:

'He don't bend!'

'Will you take his head now?' asked Seamus with a sort of exasperated patience. 'And let us be after getting a move on?'

'What if he breaks?' said Highpockets darkly.

'He will not,' said Seamus.

Highpockets put his hands under Cranley's neck and lifted,

Seamus held the ankles.

'Still don't bend, duzzy,' said Highpockets in an awed tone.

'Of course not,' said Seamus. 'He is a little stiff, there is the reason.'

'Get him inside,' snarled Father MacCord over his shoulder, interrupting a litany of call-signs he was exchanging with the door-phone.

The door opened and they trooped in.

Only the movements of his eyes betrayed the fact that Cranley was not dead. He was in fact awake, in a sense, and conscious of his surroundings. His lips were drawn back and frozen into a fair approximation of a risus sardonicus. He was speechless. Only his brain was fully active; that had more business than it could handle.

Seamus and Highpockets went up the stairs. In one place they damaged the wallpaper slightly getting Cranley's feet round a bend in the landing. They went into the debriefing room. Highpockets was for laying him on the floor. Seamus would have liked to sit him in a chair but this was out of the question as they would have had to find some way of folding him first. In the end they laid him between two chairs, one for the head and one for the feet. Highpockets said it was remarkable, something quite outside his experience. Seamus said it put him in mind of a wake. Highpockets wondered that anyone could be comfortable in such a posture. Seamus began to lose patience. Hadn't they tied James Connolly to a chair when they shot him, and him half dead already?

As they went out Father MacCord bustled in, a hypodermic in his hand. His air was businesslike. He still carried the box chained to his wrist.

He bent over Cranley with the syringe.

'Something to make you talk,' he said.

He chose a spot at random, shot the lot into the inflexible but unresisting Cranley, and went out on to the landing. From there he engaged in a shouting match with a party or parties on the ground floor. These exchanges dealt with the whereabouts, it seemed, of a key. It was clear from the rather peremptory tone of MacCord's delivery that he was anxious and more than anxious to have this key to hand as soon as might be, or, as he put it, 'fast'. However, the shadow of some obstacle had evidently fallen between this desire and its satisfaction. The argument grew hotter. Father MacCord leant further and further over the landing-banister. 'Well find it!' he shouted. 'Find it!'

He came back into the room muttering blasphemies and slammed the door behind him. He began to pace nervously up and down, rattling his chain peevishly like a man attacked by flypaper.

When he got round to noticing Cranley, he noticed that Cranley had bent: while the head and feet remained on their respective chairs, the remainder of Cranley's mass had made an accommodation with gravity to the extent of seeking a third point of support. His coccyx had come to rest on the floorboards so that a kind of equilibrium was achieved. Cranley now formed two sides of a perfect rectangle. Some of Father MacCord's ill-humour was dissipated by what he evidently regarded as a favourable change of attitude on Cranley's part.

'Can you speak?' he asked.

Cranley said that he could, thereby proving what he merely asserted—a tour de force of applied logic.

'Jolly good. Time for a little chat then,' said MacCord. With his foot he activated a tape-recorder in the next room. 'So. Tell me all about it.'

There was a pause.

'Why?' asked Cranley.

MacCord hadn't anticipated this question. Not knowing the answer, he made a reflexive dive for his beads (displacement activity). His hand was brought up short half-way to his pocket by a painful jerk of the chain. He abandoned the attempt and went back to fiddling with the chain instead.

'It's routine, Heavenspur, just routine,' he snapped. Then, more calmly and with carefully nuanced vagueness: 'Some little details, ah, might be useful. We have to have your report. . . . Don't we. It is, I believe, standard procedure in cases of this sort.'

'Is it really?' said Cranley. He was staring at the ceiling which was beginning to interest him. 'But you have the . . . whatever it is.'

'Indeed yes, ' cried Father MacCord, suddenly gay. 'We have That. In fact That is what I chiefly wanted to, ah, talk to you about.'

Cranley had found a crack on the ceiling which bore a startling resemblance to the Rappahannock River between Fredericksburg and Kelly's Ford.

'Between ourselves,' MacCord continued, 'we usually refer to it as "Q". That's confidential of course.'

Cranley said nothing.

'It stands for, ah . . .' (he thought quickly for a moment) '. . . Quintin. Or, ah, Quentin.'

'Are you sure,' said Cranley, 'you don't mean "among ourselves"? It would be less ambiguous. Not that a mistake really qualifies as an ambiguity, it's just that—'

MacCord gave a hearty chuckle and said appreciatively: 'That's good thinking, Heavenspur. Perhaps you begin to see why you were chosen for this operation. Out of so many applicants.'

'How many? About?' asked Cranley, for whom a fact without a figure was no fact.

'Ha ha,' said MacCord. 'Now listen, Heavenspur, Q has to go to Rome. The whys and wherefores don't concern you, but go it must. I think I can safely tell you that much since it's you who's, ah, taking it.'

Again Cranley said nothing. He had just withdrawn Early's brigade behind the picture rail and was moving Longstreet's corps along the plank road which led from Culpepper Court House to the main electric lamp bracket.

'So far,' MacCord continued, 'the operation has gone perfectly, but it's not over yet. The importance of bringing it to a successful . . . can hardly be . . . Our first field operation for . . . You wouldn't remember that Birmingham business? Well! I think you are beginning to appreciate the value of meticulous planning combined with strenuous training and backed by, I need hardly add, prayer. Yes, prayer, Heavenspur. The human material and the Divine Plan—an unbeatable combination, a winner every time. No need to tell you Who helps those who help themselves, eh? As the lag said to the padre, ha ha.'

He checked himself and threw Cranley a quick sideways look which Cranley missed, being unable himself to look any way but up. More soberly MacCord went on: 'Now the game's not over, Heavenspur. Not by a long, ah, chalk. It's first round to us but any relaxation at this stage is going to be premature if not fatal. We both realise that these fiends mean business and will stop at nothing. So it's up to us to fight fire with fire and carry a big stick at all times.'

'Right,' said Cranley. 'About the other thing—'

'I was coming to that, Heavenspur. I can't tell you much at the moment, of course, for security reason. But I can tell that it's going to be rough, very rough. We're embarking on the final stage now, Phase . . . ah? . . . Eight . . . Anyhow, the last lap. The procedures, though, are rather complicated just now because of certain, ah, logistical difficulties . . .' (Here he fingered the chain round his wrist) '. . . but you do your bit and we'll do ours, I can promise you that.'

Cranley threw out a cavalry screen on both sides of Cedar Run.

'About my job. You said—'

'Say no more, my dear fellow. A wink is as good as a . . . Our word is our bond, you know. Only way to do business. How are you feeling, by the way?'

'Feeling? Feeling?'

'Yes.'

'Not at all,' said Cranley, succinct.

MacCord wasn't listening. He had more important things to worry about.

'That's fine,' he said heartily. 'Fine.'

He was still worrying away at the chain. Under the continual chafing his wrist was beginning to look like a galley slave's. That idiot Felix. Maybe if he was to send Seamus for a blacksmith? He looked at his watch. Seven already. All the blacksmiths in Chiswick would likely be shut by now. What, then? Yellow pages? Locksmith? Hacksaw?

With a visible effort he dragged himself away from the matter in hand and returned to Cranley.

'I know what you're thinking, Heavenspur. You're thinking, Why doesn't he just hand over the box and let me get on with it? Well I'm sorry to have to tell you that it isn't as simple as that. Maybe when you've been in the game as long as I have you'll understand why. Nothing is as straightforward as it might seem to an outsider. Procedure is procedure. It may seem unduly complex at times, even pointless, but you may as well get it into your head right away that there's a thumping good reason for everything we do here, and the same goes for the way we do them, as you've probably heard me say before, since the way we like to do things is the RIGHT way, haven't you?'

The syntax was too much for Cranley, let alone the semantics.

'Haven't you what?' he asked fiercely.

MacCord felt the situation slipping out of his control. The only thing that remained reasonably clear was that unless and until he got this damned tin trunk off his wrist, the entire operation was going to totter over the brink on which it now stood into some awful swamp of doom, degradation, and disgrace.

To Cranley on the other hand nothing whatever was clear. The situation was fluid.

MacCord decided that if he played it by ear any longer he was going to lose contact entirely with the rest of the orchestra. Out of the corner of his eye he could see them already beginning to pack their instruments and casting significant looks towards the lifeboats. Where in God's name was Felix with that key?

'I'll ask the questions round here!' he exclaimed and in extreme agitation he suddenly dashed himself against the door and heaved it open.

'FEEEELIX!' he yelled.

There was a peripheral disturbance in his field of vision at about waist level. He looked down. Felix was kneeling on the threshold with a paintbrush between his teeth. He had the half-proud, half-guilty look of a dog who has brought in the evening paper but chewed it irremediably in the process.

MacCord began to jibber with rage and frustration.

Felix rolled his eyes desperately towards the door in a dumb appeal for understanding. The sign on the door now read:

DEBRIEFING ROOM NO I

Cranley meanwhile had taken an important decision. Having figured the odds to seven places of decimals he proposed to defend Spottsylvania Court House to the last bullet and the last drop of everyone else's blood. Armed with this pugnacious resolve, he called in his skirmishers and sat back to await the outcome.

'About my job,' he said. 'You promised. . . . You promised . . . You promised . . .'

His voice died away into a mumble. His eyes closed. He was asleep.

MacCord took in this development with silent fury, then turning to Felix he hissed poisonously between clenched lips: 'Get him out! Get him out of here before I excommunicate the whole bloody lot of you!'

They took him down to the cellar and laid him on a long table. Seamus and Highpockets did the carrying. Felix fussed about them like an over-anxious destroyer on convoy duty. MacCord remained upstairs, stomping bitterly from room to room and rattling his shackles. Finally he locked himself in the Communications Room, from which came the whir of machinery as, in a last ditch effort to redirect the frustrations that were threatening to shake him apart, he began feeding into the shredder all the paper he could lay his hands on.

He had cleared the desk and two thirds of a four-drawer filing cabinet when the fire brigade, summoned by a semi-distraught Felix, arrived with a hacksaw, just in time to save his sanity.

In the cellar Cranley slept.

# II

While they waited for Highpockets to come back, they stood around the table in the cellar and discussed the best way to set about it.

Basically it was a question of packaging. MacCord was for leaving the thing in the box. Felix opposed him. The weight of the box, he said, would add unduly to the total load and its size would make manoeuvre difficult. MacCord took the point but suggested that weight reductions might be achieved in other sectors. For example they might, instead of attaching the box to the leg as originally planned, simply remove the leg and *replace it* with the box. Felix praised this solution, calling it daring, inventive and inspired. But he begged leave to object that once the leg was off they would be left with no more than a few inches of stump to attach the plaster cast to. Seamus agreed that surgery was out what with there being no tools in the house, not so much as a hacksaw. The subject of tools was a touchy one with MacCord, but he was forced to allow that these arguments were, prima facie, incontrovertible. However, he still clung to the box. It went without saying, he said, that its contents were too precious to be subjected to all the natural shocks, etc.

At this point, Felix returned to the attack. What was needed was a rigid container, right? Well, a plaster cast was a rigid container or was it not? Seamus, whose opinion had not been asked, said that in his opinion it was. That was what a plaster cast was, a rigid container. Felix waxed eloquent in defence of his thesis and MacCord eventually conceded the point; but he held out for some form of protective covering to intervene between the plaster, viewed as a container, and the thing it was to contain.

The latter was variously referred to in the course of the conversation as 'it', 'the whatsit', 'the gri-gri' (Felix), and—by Father

MacCord, when he remembered—as 'Q' or, more familiarly, 'Quentin'.

Seamus now said that he had the very thing for the job. A polythene bag, that was your man. MacCord was doubtful at first, Felix enthusiastic. Seamus dashed upstairs for the bag, a fine big one in which his Sunday suit had just returned from the cleaner's. He showed it to them proudly. It had SPEEDY CLEANERS written across it in large red letters.

The bag was elected by a unanimous vote.

Cranley did not vote, being asleep.

Highpockets came back with twenty yards of plaster bandage and they set to work.

# 12

Miss Thirkell presented herself on demand before Father Mac-Cord in Father MacCord's office. She seemed nervous, flustered, and she became more so when MacCord told her to put away her notebook as there would be no dictation that day. He did his best to put her at her ease: he patted her, he placed her in his best chair, he fussed around her like a whole team of chefs round a gargantuan soufflé; he offered her a cigarette, coffee, tea, his views on the weather, a handful of well-turned compliments, and the chance to strike a blow in defence of Mother Church, in that order.

Miss Thirkell's agitation grew.

It was, indeed, a state natural with her, but subject to fluctuations which, if plotted on a graph, would present a seemingly random pattern. But in reality, the frequency, intensity and duration of the quantum shifts in Miss Thirkell's agitation levels were directly related to the hostility content of her perceived environment. Waking or sleeping, she viewed the cosmos from an attitude which may be described as Taut. The hostility factor approached, but never reached, zero, and her mental state, even in moments of repose in secure environments, never attained total tranquillity. Her world was a glasshouse peopled by maniacs with catapults.

MacCord addressed her in accents of vibrant paternalism.

'My dear young lady, do you know what day this is?'

'Wednesday?' said Miss Thirkell tentatively.

Half of her *knew* it was Wednesday as she had picked up the 'Woman's Own' on her way to work. The other half of her, suddenly, Doubted.

'It is D-Day,' said MacCord with the satisfied smile of a man who has just bestowed half a sovereign on the Deserving Poor.

Miss Thirkell's hand flew to her mouth holding a tiny square of lace-trimmed cambric, much twisted, representing a handkerchief.

'Oh dear,' she said. 'D-Day.'

'Yes. And the time,' MacCord pursued, pleased with impact he was having, 'is H minus five.'

Miss Thirkell gasped.

'Yes,' said MacCord. 'H minus five, already.'

At this point there formed in Miss Thirkell's mind the sudden and quite definite conviction that his next question was going to be, 'What is green, has vertical stripes, and goes up and down?' She tried to concentrate on remembering the solution. A rabbit on a motor bike? No, not that. Moby Plum? A partridge in a pear tree?

'Oh dear,' she said again.

She looked at her watch. It was pinned to her blouse. MacCord's eyes followed the gesture.

'You are right, my dear. There is no time to be lost, or, ah, very little. You have a passport of course.'

'Not . . . with me. At home.'

'Bad, bad, bad. Time is of the essence. It must be fetched. And quickly.' He snapped down an intercom button on his desk. 'Car!' he cried.

There was no answer.

'Car!' he cried again, louder, bending over and peering into the machine as if to get a closer look at someone or something caged behind the speaker grille.

'There's . . . no answer,' said Miss Thirkell.

'There isn't, is there?' said MacCord.

'Usually,' said Miss Thirkell, wringing her hands, 'I answer.'

'Hum?' said MacCord, puzzled. Then: 'Ha!'

'And I'm . . . in here,' said Miss Thirkell as bashfully as if confessing to a shameful disease.

'Exactly. Here you are, my dear. Here you are. So! *And where is my car?*'

Coming on top of the accumulated uncertainties of the last ten minutes, this outburst, though mild, brought the already tottering edifice of Miss Thirkell's composure crashing into total ruin.

She began to cry.

Miss Thirkell in tears was something seismic. Her entire anatomy was abandoned to a series of tremors, counter-tremors, primary and secondary shock waves, concussions, percussions, repercussions, heaves, ripples, gasping, tsunami and general turmoil. No part of her surface area was unaffected and Mac-Cord was in a subdued frenzy.

Whipping out a large handkerchief hand holding it in front of him like a flag of truce, he took a step forward. 'For Heaven's sake, Miss Thirkell. Your—' He stopped suddenly when he realised what he had been going to say. 'Your bosom is heaving,' he had been going to say . . . He took a number of deep breaths, very efficacious against panic, and gripped his rosary firmly, balling it up in his fist till the beads squeaked against each other. He withdrew the handkerchief and mopped his own face with it.

It took another ten minutes of his precious time to restore Miss Thirkell to a kind of precarious calm, and a further half hour to explain exactly what it was he wanted her to do.

It was not until they were almost at the airport that he had soothed the last of her hesitations and tutted away the last of her fears.

# 13

Cranley smiled in his sleep. He dreamt he was in an aeroplane with Miss Thirkell.

His dream was testimony of an improved grip on reality for he really was in an aeroplane and Miss Thirkell was in the seat next to him. Some fifteen hours of unbroken sleep had brought him nearer to normalcy than he had been at any time since the beginning of his Field Training, four and a half days previously. But even now enough of the assorted drugs that had been pumped into him remained unmetabolised in his bloodstream to people his mind with regiments, squadrons and batteries endlessly manoeuvring along dotted lines on a labyrinthine chessboard. Or at times the space behind his eyes would fill with tremendous projections of what looked like logarithmic tables, column upon column, row upon row, the marching matrices stretching to the limits of his vision. And behind it all, voices, mechanically repeating the same message, over and over, as if reading from a book which said the same thing on every page: 'In an n-person zero-sum game the assignment of utilities is subject to a geometric increase in complexity of the order of n to the n minus one'. . . .

In his sleep he reached out and took Miss Thirkell's hand.

Miss T., as already stated, was neurotically averse to being touched. She contemplated the imprisoned member with a certain anxiety.

Her first reaction was to disengage, but Cranley's grasp was firm and if she pulled hard she might wake him. Father Mac-Cord, it was true, had assured her that Heavenspur was dead to the world and could be counted on to remain that way for the duration of the 'mission'. Indeed, it was, as he had explained, the very fact of Heavenspur's untimely flirtation with Morpheus that had made her own presence necessary. Heavenspur could hardly wheel himself around in his sleep, ha ha. He might, ha ha, get run over. And of course, MacCord had explained reassuringly, a quasi-permanently somnolent Heavenspur was in no condition to revert to the lamentable behaviour that had led to the little, ah, contretemps, in the Statuary Stockroom. On that score she need have no fears. She surely did not for a moment imagine that he (MacCord) would for a moment entertain the notion of her (Miss Thirkell's) going along if there were the remotest danger of his (Heavenspur's) renewing his odious, ah, attentions? And if, impossibly, the worst should come to the worst, she retained the option of flight, at a brisk walking pace —no particular exertion being required to put ground between herself and a man with forty pounds of plaster on his leg. MacCord permitted himself to doubt whether Heavenspur could so much as stand, let alone indulge in mad pursuit of maidens loth. Poor fellow.

Miss Thirkell jumped when the p/a system crackled suddenly into her ear. 'This is your Captain speaking' in broken English. All passengers who were in a position to do so could, by looking out of the windows on the port side, see the Island of Elba, over which they were now passing. The passengers craned obediently to the windows on both sides of the aircraft. Half of them saw nothing and some resentment was felt here and there. The other half, on the lucky side, saw the island, or rather the heap of cloud which marked its position. Miss Thirkell was the only one to see a lonely macaroon stranded on an enormous blue plate. A touch of poetry in her nature.

She looked away from the window to Cranley. She looked down at her trapped hand. She looked at Cranley's massive leg sticking out into the aisle, a menace to shipping. She remembered her own legs and with her free hand she smoothed her skirt—an automatic gesture, and unnecessary as her knees were well covered. As she did so her hand brushed against the plaster cast. A feeling almost like an electric shock ran through her fingers, up her arm and invaded her body, settling somewhere deep in her stomach. It was a feeling like no feeling she had ever felt before. It was Funny. She didn't like it at all. She jerked her hand away, settled back in her seat and Tried To Be Calm.

The Captain's voice came again. Miss Thirkell jumped again. In half an hour they would be landing. 'Italy,' thought Miss Thirkell with a little tingle in her palms. . . .

The agitation centred on the point where Cranley and Miss Thirkell sat so cosily together at the front of the tourist-class cabin, being largely psychic—more of an aura than a disturbance—offered no special features to catch the roving eye of the stewardess who was standing in her On Watch position at the back of the cabin, slightly behind the rearmost row of seats. She was competent, resourceful and well-groomed; her attractively-proportioned young body was exactly tailored to fit the contours of her smart grey suit; her skin-deep smile was in a constant state of Green Alert, to be brought instantly into play when needed; her home was at Como, birthplace of Alessandro Volta (1745-1827). She had blonde hair, worn short, and brown eyes. Her name was Fiammetta and her telephone number was a much-sought-after secret.

From where she stood her bird's eye was free to scan the hair and hats of the passengers arrayed in front of her like so many shelves of groceries. Experience had developed and sharpened to a fine point her ability to tell from no more than a glance at any given occiput whether or not its owner required her services and, if so, which service—coffee, milk, tea, cushion, paper bag, help with seat belt, reassurance, No. 1 smile, No. 2 smile, boiled sweet, or directions for reaching the toilet. Thus she had correctly diagnosed the intermittent all-azimuths rotation of Miss Thirkell's headpiece as mild nervous excitement—action required: none. Her companion, too, was in some respects a model passenger: as he had been asleep during, since, and probably before boarding, his state approached, and in fact wildly exceeded, the degree of inertia which, from the professional point of view, constituted ideal passenger-behaviour. On the other hand, it had taken four men to get him on board, and unloading him might present some headaches. Furthermore, the swollen bulk of his plaster leg, obtruding into the aisle, caused a partial obstruction and had brought complaints from one or two finicky travellers that it inspired Morbid Thoughts and

146

might it not be covered with a rug?

However, the logistical and aesthetic problems posed by Cranley's leg were in no way the cause of lovely Fiammetta's present headache.

The Chinaman was driving her crazy.

# 14

The morning's meeting had lasted an hour and three quarters. It had started with Reports. Then followed a snap test on Doctrine and Dogma, with a heavy emphasis on Damnable Errors. The Cardinals had staggered through this somehow; there was one serious mishap—when Cardinal Fegato, called on to name seven Gnostic sects, had dried up at six. Balai-Rose had saved the day by supplying the seventh: Antitactae.

So far so good. These quiz sessions, increasingly frequent of late, were an added strain, but the Cardinals were coming to accept them as a normal, if unpleasant, part of their daily business.

The next item on the agenda turned out to be a harangue or sermon on the theme, 'Error Has No Rights', delivered from the Chair.

The Good News comes last, in three parts.

1. Paper Bag had already entered its final phase. The Document would be arriving in Rome by special courier that very afternoon.

2. Once it was safely in their hands, the situation, or, as Polenta termed it, the 'balance of forces' would be changed out of all recognition. It would be open to them, with this new weapon at their disposal, to return to the struggle with renewed vigour and confidence and rapidly bring matters to the consummation they all so devoutly wished. The word 'showdown' was mentioned in this connection.

3. The decks being cleared for action by the success of Paper Bag, there was no further obstacle to the Prosecution of Project New Broom. Operations Section had been instructed to draw up a revised schedule for the Final, Pre-Final and Pre-Pre-Final phases of New Broom. A countdown would be started at 18.00 hours.

When he left the meeting Polenta was in high good humour. 'That'll give them something to think about,' he was thinking. 'Keep them on their toes.' And tomorrow he would give them something more to think about: he would tell them about the List.

But the Cardinals, left behind in the Committee Room, were anything but on their toes after this latest bombshell had left a crater in their already uncertain morale. Indeed, they were sagging in their chairs around the long table like so many sacks of cold porridge. Quenched, they were, to a man. Chingada, for one, was close to tears.

In the corridor Polenta was intercepted by a Chamberlain. His Holiness begged the favour of a few moments of Cardinal Polenta's time.

'When?' asked Polenta ungraciously.

'At once, Eminence.'

Polenta classed this event as Bad News. He had better things to do right now, and barely enough time in which to do them. His elation dropped several notches.

'Ah, Cardinal Polenta,' said H.H. when the Chairman had duly presented himself. 'There is something we wish to take up with you. We think it is only fair to tell you that we have been talking to Cardinal Nuvoletto. About the work of your Committee.'

This information caused a sudden frantic flurry of gear changes in Polenta's mental processes. In the first place it seemed highly improbable that anyone could have been talking to Nuvoletto about anything at all, given that Nuvoletto was deaf as a post. And if it was true, the fat might really be in the fire. The old buffer might have blown the entire operation.

'Ah,' said Polenta guardedly.

'A charming person,' H.H. continued. 'Quite charming. So . . . wise. Don't you think?'

'My own opinion exactly, Holiness,' mumbled Polenta.

'Such discernment. A refined judgement to match his venerable years. He must be a great help to you in your work?'

'Oh, indubitably,' said Polenta. He didn't like the look of this at all.

There was a pause. H.H. seemed uncertain how to proceed. He spent some moments chewing his lower lip. The eyes behind his spectacles moved erratically to and fro in search of something to focus on, like indecisive motorists hunting for a parking space.

'Cardinal Polenta, your Committee has been deliberating for . . . how long now?'

Polenta, scenting a subterfuge, was unwilling to commit himself to a definite figure. 'For some time,' he said.

'Quite so,' said H.H. 'We have been giving a great deal of thought lately to certain . . . Well . . . In view of the forthcoming Council . . .'

Polenta gave a start. The Council! Warning bells began to ring in his head, red lights flashed.

'We have been thinking recently that if one could . . . as it were . . . present the Council with . . . shall we say . . . with a fait accompli . . . so to speak.'

Polenta nearly choked. Was the man a mind reader? Or worse?

'So we took the liberty of discussing a few proposals with Cardinal Nuvoletto.'

Polenta was unable to hide his startled surprise. H.H. saw this and went on hurriedly.

'Oh, please don't think for a moment that we have been in any sense . . . haha . . . plotting behind your back. . . .' (Exactly what Polenta did think. H.H. and Nuvoletto together. Thick as thieves.) 'It's simply that we were unwilling to add to the burdens you already bear.' H.H. looked at Polenta to see how he was taking it and then looked quickly away again. 'We hoped you would understand. What with the recent unrest in the South American provinces . . .'

The more Polenta heard, the less he liked what he heard. Until this moment he had regarded the unrest in the South American provinces as strictly his own preserve.

'We see that surprises you,' H.H. continued. 'Oh some of them are *very* discontented, we fear. What is needed is something concrete, concrete evidence that the Church is alive to the least as well as the greatest of her children's perplexities. And we look to you, Cardinal Polenta, to help us provide that evidence.'

'Evidence, Your Holiness?' In Polenta's vocabulary this was a charged word, pregnant.

'Yes,' said H.H. definitely. 'Specific remedies for specific grievances, that's the ticket.'

Polenta agreed dumbly.

'It is, it is,' said H.H., gaining confidence and momentum. 'No doubt about it. So we turn to you, Polenta. Now . . . To business. Cardinal Nuvoletto has assured us that you have something up your sleeve, as it were. Something big, by all accounts.'

Betrayed? Betrayed! Polenta's mouth dropped open.

'Ah, you see,' pursued H.H. gaily. 'We know your little secret, Polenta. . . . So what is it?'

Polenta took a step back. A pit had been digged for him, yawning at his feet.

He said: 'But!'

'Come now,' H.H. chided him. 'No reticences, please. After all, it touches our own interests, does it not?'

Polenta just stared at him. His mind had frozen into a kind of grey lump.

H.H. contemplated as much as he could see of Polenta's reactions with an indulgent smile.

'Your modesty does you credit. You had thought to surprise us, perhaps, with your little schemes?'

Polenta opened his mouth for a denial but only a sort of strangling noise came out.

'There's no point in denying it,' H.H. said. 'We have always known there were hidden depths to you. Come now . . . Why try to hide things this way? . . . It's the tropical uniforms, isn't it?'

Tropical uniforms, tropical uniforms, tropical—the words went round and round in Polenta's head, meaninglessly. He repeated the phrase to himself as if it was a foreign language. His face wore the stunned look of a man who has just forgotten his own name.

'You see,' said H.H. 'We knew all along. You had perhaps forgotten that we had a hand in their design.' He caught the expression on Polenta's face and began to feel a touch of alarm at the way his little piece of banter was turning out. His voice took on a note of anxious solicitude.

'It was to have been a surprise, of course. If it wasn't for the urgency of the . . . Nothing was further from our mind than to . . . You're not . . . angry, Polenta?'

Polenta took a big breath and let it out slowly.

'No,' he croaked. It was the best that he could do for the moment.

'It's marvellous news,' H.H. assured him, 'coming at this time. Marvellous.'

He felt a sudden desire to do something nice for Polenta, to reward him in some way.

'Cardinal Polenta, this afternoon we are giving an audience to inaugurate our Week of Prayer for the Physically Handicapped. A specially selected group. It is another of our projects which is very close to our heart. A new departure, almost . . . We would be greatly pleased if you would consent to attend. Assist with the rites and so forth?'

He ended on a note of interrogation, his spectacles glinting benignly as he waited for Polenta's reply. And, as if from another room, Polenta seemed to hear himself say: 'I should be greatly honoured, Your Holiness.'

# 15

Chang's behaviour had attracted the notice (unfavourable) of the stewardess Fiammetta from the moment of his first boarding the aircraft.

He had tried to leave his seat fourteen times during the first eleven minutes of the flight. Fiammetta had kept count.

She had kept him in his seat. This had taken some doing.

The first time he tried it the aircraft still had one foot on the ground. She had slapped him down with a heavy-duty smile while he was still fumbling with the buckle of his seat-belt. She jerked the belt tight with a skilful one-handed gesture that, while seeming casual, was both polite and firm. With the other hand she aimed a spiky finger culminating in a pointed, polished and painted fingernail at the illuminated sign which said FASTEN SEAT BELTS. There was one of these above each seat. Nipped in the bud, Chang subsided, but the moment her back was turned he was at it again. She caught him in time, checked his fastenings, and threw in an extra boiled sweet for good measure.

The next time she added a pillow, a travelling rug and two copies of 'La Stampa'. Chang still didn't give up. It seemed that every time the stewardess looked over her shoulder, there he was, dumbly and desperately wrestling with his seat belt.

It developed into a full-blown People's Liberation Struggle.

In the end he had to give it up. The simplicity of the release mechanism was too much for his devious oriental mind. Furthermore, although he was sitting at the very back of the cabin, his duel with the Stewardess was beginning to attract the attention of the other passengers (the last thing he wanted) and it was obvious from the admiring looks she was getting whose side they were on.

This new alignment of forces placed Chang in a position where further resistance must involve him in a head-on clash with Authority backed by Public Opinion. The outcome could only be Loss of Face, automatic and massive. Chang scores minus ten and loses the game.

Unthinkable.

He began to cast about for something thinkable.

Fast, clear, ordered thinking comes hard to a man who, after a long series of humiliating reverses, has gambled life, career and reputation on a single desperate cast of fortune. And now is sitting in an aeroplane at five thousand feet with a pair of live hand-grenades burning holes in his jacket pockets.

The effort of cerebration kept him almost immobile for nearly seventeen minutes. Fiammetta began cautiously to count her chickens.

'He hasn't moved for seventeen minutes,' she said to the second stewardess when they met briefly in the little pantry full of half-eaten plastic lunches.

The second stewardess, in the middle of a hasty re-lipsticking, gave her a thumbs-up sign. A buzzer buzzed. Fiammetta looked up at the tell-tale board.

'It's him,' she said. 'In culo.'

'A li mortacci sua,' said the second stewardess.

'Have you seen his teeth?' said Fiammetta with a little shudder.

Chang looked up at her, smiling, calm, benevolent. A changed man.

'Bring me,' he said grandly, 'a map.'

'Mappa?'

'A large map,' said Chang.

'Mappa,' repeated the stewardess, frowning. 'Mappa? Ah! Grappa!'

Chang's face fell like a sky-diver with a badly-packed parachute. Glappa?

'No,' he cried. And then: 'One moment please. Wait.'

He dived into his briefcase and came up with a rainbow-coloured booklet called 'Get around in fifteen languages'. He began a hurricane consultation. He had torn out a good third of the pages when he finally gave a yelp of triumph.

'Carta!' he cried, waving the ravaged enchiridion under

Fiammetta's nose. 'Carte. Karte. MAP!'

'Ah!' said Fiammetta. 'Carte.'

'Yes. Map,' agreed Chang. He nodded with a vigour that made his teeth click.

She leaned across, took a shiny paper folder from the seat pocket and held it out to him.

'Ecco,' she said.

Chang snatched at it. Before you could say I Resolve To Overfulfil My Work Norms he had the map spread out on his knees while the remaining contents of the folder—post cards, safety instructions, catalogue of duty-free perfumes—were scattered to the four winds.

As maps go it was a fine map, custom-built for the armchair dictator. From Great Britain in the top left-hand corner to the Bay of Naples, bottom right, it was all there. But as maps go that was as far as it went: Prestwick to Pompeii. For the co-ordinates of the Trobriand Islands or the distance in versts from Bokhara to Kizil Bak a person would have to look elsewhere.

Chang ran a feverish finger over the red lines which connected London to Rome by a variety of routes, some direct, some downright devious. His index dodged drunkenly among the major nodes of the West European air-traffic network. Whichever way he tried it, he ended up in London or Rome. A topological impasse.

Before long his face had gone as pale as it possibly could and his nose and forehead were covered with minute drops of sweat, one to each pore. He looked up and tried to speak. On the first attempt he only managed a croak. The second time, in a voice like death, he said: 'It's not here.'

'No?' said Fiammetta with simulated surprise.

'Here,' said Chang. He waved his hand in the air which bordered the eastern edge of the map—a gesture Columbus must have seen a hundred times from people telling him, Look, this is where you go over.

'Here it is,' said Chang. 'Here.' The stewardess leaned nearer to see. 'But it isn't. So where is it?'

'Where is what?' she asked. Not that she cared.

Chang seemed not to be ready for this particular question. Perhaps the bluntness of it upset him. He fiddled with his collar and thought hard before answering. Then, glancing cautiously all about him, he signalled her to lean closer and into her ear he whispered hoarsely: 'Albania.'

'Albania,' said the stewardess. She looked at the map. 'It's not there,' she said. 'It's here.' And in her turn she waved her hand in the air where the Balkan peninsula would have been.

'Exactly,' said Chang. 'Precisely. That is exactly where it is and it is not there. Bring me please another map.'

'I'm sorry,' she said. 'There isn't any other map.'

'This is the only map? Impossible.'

'All the other maps are the same.'

'What,' exclaimed Chang. 'No Belgrade? No Sofia? No—???' Instead of finishing the phrase he turned on her, a piercing glance surmounted by a pair of eyebrows at maximum elevation. This put the ball squarely in her court.

'No Athens,' she supplied. 'All the same like this one.'

'No Athens? No—???'

Again the interrogative look.

'All the same,' she said. 'Like this one.'

Chang mopped his brow with the sleeve of his high-collared jacket and did some more thinking. Dead end. So go back and try again. But try what? He could . . . No. Or he could. . . . Hardly. Or . . . !

An inspiration.

'I want to send a telegram.'

'Now? From here?'

'That's right,' said Chang. 'Yes. A telegram.' He did a little mime of a man tapping a morse key.

Fiammetta considered him thoughtfully, trying to gauge the risk of disappointing him. In the end she temporised.

'Just a moment please,' she said and went away.

Chang took out a pencil.

Fiammetta retreated to her pantry and rang through to the flight deck. 'Si si, vuol mandare un telegramma, 'sto coso. . . . Si, un telegramma. . . . Eh, lo so, ma lui mi sembra suonato. . . .

Tenerlo buono? È da Londra che lo tengo buono . . . OK . . . Va bene.' She hung up wearily. She glanced in the mirror, straightened her slumping shoulders, and returned to chez Chang. Normally, she told him, they didn't accept telegrams in flight. But she had explained to the radio officer how important it was—('Vital,' agreed Chang emphatically)—and she was permitted to make an exception. The company put the wishes of the passengers before all others, etc. . . . Before she could finish her buttered address Chang was thrusting into her hand a mauled and grubby sheet on which he had pencilled his message. She took it and turned to go. Chang clutched at her sleeve.

'Wait. You haven't read it. You must read first to be sure that it is clear.' He was pleading as a drowning man might plead with a monkey whom he knows to have access to a lifebelt.

For the first time some of the pathos of Chang's frustration penetrated the outer crust of Fiammetta's professional aloofness. But instead of making her more sympathetic to his plight—at this point she might, for example, have made a genuine effort to find out what was bothering him—it brought her carefully suppressed resentment to the surface in a hot flash of anger that all but melted her mascara. She came, perhaps, as near to an act of battery against a passenger as she had done at any time in her career.

But training won, and dutifully she went through the motions of reading the 'telegram'. Humour him, she repeated grimly. Humour him.

The message read:

ARRIVING ROME THIS AFTERNOON
CAN YOU MEET ME LOVE WILLIAM

'It's for my aunt,' Chang explained.

'It's very well,' said Fiammetta. 'But you realise it will arrive to your aunt only after we will reach Roma?'

Chang jabbed at the paper with his pencil.

'The address,' he hissed.

The telegram was addressed to:

Reading this Fiammetta began to realise she should have left well alone. Now she was committed to making at least a token attempt at getting the telegram sorted out.

'This . . . Ulinov Trg, is in Roma?'

'No,' replied Chang with the beginnings of a triumphant smile. He permitted himself a whisper of exultation at the success of his ruse. 'It is in . . . Albania!' And he added, in a voice so pregnant with meaning that it sagged like a paper bag full of marmalade: 'The *capital* of Albania.'

'Capital. Va bene. It is still so that when you already are in Roma this telegram still hasn't arrived to your aunt in . . .'

'Yes!' cried Chang. Then: 'Yes?' He urged her on, smiting his fist into his palm.

'In Albania,' she said.

'In the c a p i t a l of Albania,' moaned Chang.

'Yes,' she said. 'In . . .'

'In? In? In?'

'Mmmmmmma . . . in Tirana, so that she has not the possibility to arrange—'

A storm of fireworks burst over the night in Chang's mind.

Joy, Relief, Triumph, Hope, Exultation, Enthusiasm and Determination chased each other across his features so rapidly that for a space of several seconds his face was actually reduced to a blur, while his eyes, in perfect synchrony, Glowed, Gleamed, Glittered, Shone, Sparkled, Glinted and Flashed Defiantly to match the prevailing mood.

The startled Fiammetta, sole witness of this unparallelled piece of facial gymnastics, was recalled from a trance of awestruck contemplation by a sharp pricking sensation in her left palm.

'Ai!' she said.

'Write,' commanded Chang, pressing the pencil more firmly into her hand and closing her fingers round it.

'Write what?' she asked him.

'The name. The name for the address. Tilana.'

As if she was obeying a post-hypnotic command she bent down, rested the paper on the arm of the seat, and in the catastrophic scrawl that in Italy passes for calligraphy she wrote—

*Tirana, A 1—*

Before she could finish, the paper was snatched from her hand. Chang had exploded into movement and the Great Seat-Belt Battle was on again.

'Get me out. Get me out,' he gasped.

Automatically she put her hands against his shoulders and started to push him back into the seat. Suddenly he stopped struggling and went limp. Caught unawares she fell a little towards him so that her right ear was brought close enough to Chang's mouth to feel the draught of his hoarse and menacing whisper:

'Undo this belt at once. If I do not go to the toilet IMMEDI-ATELY, there will be an Unfortunate Accident.'

The decision to utter this threat had been taken without conscious thought on Chang's part. The phrase 'unfortunate accident', in particular, had been supplied by his subconscious and originated, not in the coy periphrases of potty training, but in a favourite threat of Chang's hero Jack the Duke, viz:

> Get your hands up high, gentlemen,
> and no sudden moves please, or
> there's liable to be an . . . etc.

But for the stewardess these words conjured up a whole gamut of nauseating mishaps, the kind that constitute a standing night-mare among the occupational hazards of her profession. With-out thinking twice she flicked up the tab on the buckle and Chang was free.

It took him perhaps half a second to digest the fact. During this time he sat as if shot, staring down at what had happened to the belt.

Then he was out of his seat and away up the aisle so fast and so suddenly that he left Fiammetta reeling back against the door of her pantry and a hole in space where he had been.

Barrelling along between the seats like a small meteor he reached the end of the cabin, hopped over Cranley's leg without breaking his stride, and was through the first-class cabin between two sips of champagne. Before a head anywhere had time to complete a turn towards the source of the disturbance, he was gone and left nothing behind to mark his wake but the flapping of the curtains through which he had passed.

He found himself in a kind of vestibule contained by four doors: behind him the curtained entrance to the first-class cabin; on his left the outer door of the plane; on his right a door over which shone the sign TOILET VACANT; and finally, dead ahead, the door to the flight deck.

Chang skidded to a stop.

At this point anyone privy to Chang's diabolical intentions might be entitled to predict his next move with some confidence: he is going to effect an illicit irruption into the Command Centre by way of the door to his immediate front. This door is marked:

CREW ONLY

STRICTLY NO ADMITTANCE

but this is not, one feels, going to stop Comrade Chang in his present state.

However. . . .

He was not alone in the vestibule.

A moment before Chang's entry from the lower or passenger end, the second stewardess had emerged from the flight deck hotfoot from a rumbustious five minutes at the controls of Gianfranco, the co-pilot. Having closed the door behind her she availed herself of the privacy the vestibule afforded to make some lightning repairs to her disordered clothing. With a movement so practised as to be almost reflexive she bent forward, flicked her skirt up over her waist and slipped her hands up under the waistband from below. From this position she could get a purchase on the hem of her blouse, which had come loose, and pull it back into her skirt.

This was the moment chosen by Chang to make his whirl-wind entrance, and from this point matters proceeded with the smoothness of a well-rehearsed ballet and as inevitably as the days of the week.

Chang, thunderstruck, pulled up dead an inch short of collision point. The stewardess, bent double, had started instinctively to straighten up even before the awareness of an intruding presence had had time to penetrate the upper levels of her consciousness. Thus it was that with the precision of a trapeze act the chin of the decelerating Chang entered the exact point in space about to be occupied, a split second later, by the cranium of the straightening stewardess.

The blow on the jaw he received turned the world black and, still impelled by a remnant of inertial momentum, he stumbled and sagged forward on top of his assailant. The stewardess found her equilibrium seriously threatened, but in her haste to unbend she had succeeded in trapping her hands in the waist-band of her skirt and so was denied the use of her arms in her efforts to keep her balance. The situation was without remedy, for Chang, in a punch-drunk gesture of self preservation, had wrapped his arms about her, pinioning her own. Meanwhile his weight was dragging her down.

Locked together like clumsy lovers they sank sideways and downwards. Their combined weight crashed against the flimsy door of the toilet and they sank to the floor inside.

Chang's blackout was only partial and temporary. Within a few seconds awareness was beginning to return. In the mean-time the stewardess, winded and also slightly groggy from the blow on her head, had construed the event as an assault on her honour. She therefore kept up a vigorous struggle of which the only concrete result was the slamming of the toilet door behind them, so that when Chang came to, it was to find him-self one of a pair of dazed and desperate people apparently wrestling each other to death in a space no larger than the average broom cupboard.

It did not help that he was suffering from a kind of schizoid vision which made him see two different situations simultaneously, or the same situation from two different points of view, or possibly even two different halves of the same situation. One part of his mind saw that he had somehow strayed from the execution of the plan as originally conceived. At the same time another part of him seemed to know, as if he had just been told it, or had just read it somewhere, that he had reached the end of the line and if the plan was to be put into operation at all, it was Now or Never. It was as though this part of his mind had managed to avoid getting locked in the toilet, had skipped over or round the whole unfortunate business and was even now standing masterfully on the flight deck, a grenade in either hand, while the terrified and cringing crewmen bent themselves like putty to his majestic purposes.

So as the stewardess collapsed across the lavatory bowl and proceeded to go into a fit of screaming hysterics, Chang took a grenade from either pocket and, shaking them under her nose, began to shout: 'FLY TO TILANA YOU DOGS OR I'LL BLOW US ALL TO SMITHELEENS.'

And a few seconds later the plane touched down at Fiumicino.

# 16

The white bus was on the last leg of its long journey from the south.

It had stopped the previous evening at Terracina, eighty miles south of Rome on Highway Seven, the Via Appia. Overnight accommodation was arranged for the passengers in a monastery. They had meant to make an early start the next morning, but embarkation had been, as usual, a lengthy business.

By midday they had crossed the Pontine Marshes and were at Cisterna on the southern slopes of the Alban Hills. Half an hour later, the other side of Albano, they had their first sight of their goal, the Eternal City spread like a grey fungus across the horizon.

On the downhill run the driver, scenting home, quickened his pace. His instructions were to drive carefully, for his cargo was precious. But now caution was forgotten as the passengers, intoxicated by a heady cocktail of holiday spirit and religious fervour urged him on with excited cries. The pick of the bunch they were, from all over southern Italy, selected by precise criteria rigorously applied. Many of the participants had given their life savings for a place.

No wonder then that excitement grew among them as they drew within sight of their journey's end.

# 17

Miss Thirkell's instructions were simple. On arrival in Rome she was to make her way to St Peter's Square by means of the highways tending in that direction. There she was to ask for the Via Adolfo Muni. In the Via Adolfo Muni there was a pasticceria, anglice, a spaghetti shop. She was to go to the shop and wait until someone told her what to do next.

She got as far as St Peter's Square without any serious mishap, but by the time she got there she was dangerously overwrought.

Some of the factors making for overwroughtness in Miss Thirkell have already been mentioned—chronic inability to relax, the mysterious circumstances of her mission, excitement at the prospect of foreign travel, natural apprehension as to what might occur if Mr Heavenspur should wake up, and so forth. These forces combined to create a situation which any additional aggravation might bring to a crisis point.

The first additional jolt had come with the business of the Chinaman. Very upsetting that had been. As they were landing she had heard screams coming from the front end of the plane. Then she had seen from her porthole a fleet of ambulances, fire engines and police cars with bells ringing, lights flashing and sirens wailing, converge on them from all parts of the airfield. Then there had been crashes and shouts and she had seen a young woman in stewardess's uniform led away from the plane. A few moments later they had brought out the Chinaman. There was a whole crowd of people round him helping him—policemen, firemen with axes, and men in white coats carrying first-aid equipment. The poor man was struggling and jumping about like anything, obviously terribly upset. He seemed to have got his arms caught up in the long sleeves of the white jacket he was wearing. They had put him into an ambulance—rather roughly, Miss Thirkell thought—and driven him away very fast. After that everything was quiet again. Miss Thirkell asked the stewardess what was happening. It was nothing to worry about, the stewardess said. One of the passengers had fainted in the toilet. She said it as though that sort of thing happened quite normally.

Miss Thirkell had no way of knowing how far these incidents were a normal feature of air travel. It is certain that the extra excitement did her nerves no good.

Getting poor Mr Heavenspur off the plane had been a bit wearing, too. In the end they had put him, chair and all, on one of those little electric carts they put the baggage in, and carried him into the airport building. How embarrassed he would have been if he could have seen himself!

Her own troubles started later, after the bus had taken them into the city and dropped them at the air terminal.

Father MacCord had explained that to get from the air terminal to St Peter's she would have to go right across the centre of the city. She meant to take a taxi. Father MacCord had said it was all right to do that. Expense was no object on this trip, he had said. But there were no taxis to be had. She found a taxi-driver who spoke English of a sort and explained where she wanted to go. He had replied, as far as she could understand, that it was fine with him, he would take her anywhere. He knew all the best places. But there was no question of including Mr Heavenspur in the party. His taxi too was small, he said, giving her some funny looks. In the end he got quite huffy about it and drove off. The other taxi drivers were all the same. They were more than willing to take her anywhere—some even offered to make the trip free of charge as a gesture of Anglo-Italian understanding—but Mr Heavenspur was out. Their taxis were too small.

In the end she had to walk.

Little demons of apprehension and excitement turned cartwheels in her guts as she set off. Small wonder. It was no stroll she had undertaken, but a trek.

The wheelchair was heavy and difficult to manoeuvre at the best of times: now she had to cope with streets which were thick with motor vehicles in the care of maniacs whose psychological disorders ranged from cheerful irresponsibility to homicidal frenzy; and with pavements that groaned under an overload of anarchically-inclined pedestrians swarming in every direction except the straightforward to and fro for which the sidewalks were designed.

After a few yards she stopped, took out the street map Mac-Cord had given her, and fixed it with a safety pin to the collar of Cranley's coat. In this way she could follow the map while keeping both hands free for the chair.

She had not gone very far before it became clear: (a) that Miss Thirkell was the worst possible person to have sent to Rome, and (b) that Rome was the worst possible place to have sent her. In the first place Miss Thirkell was an attractive young woman, even, to some men, irresistible. As we have seen. But *all* attractive young women are irresistible to *all* Italian men. Secondly, there is an exuberant vulgarity about city-bred Italians and a cheerful absence of sensitivity and taste in their social behaviour. Perhaps if it were otherwise they would be unable to live with one another. But in their dealings with strangers in their midst this lack of restraint can become total.

The spectacle, therefore, of an attractive but harassed young lady struggling, in broad daylight, with an invalid chair complete with invalid (and the latter unconscious to boot)—was too much. A sight which in London would hardly have turned a single head, which in Paris would have caused no more than an evanescent stir, and which in Berlin would have given rise at most to a mild sense of outrage, in Rome had all the makings of a movable riot.

Miss Thirkell soon collected about her a small but enthusiastic group of adherents, assistants, commentators and detractors—some content with disinterested observation, others shouting wildly contradictory advice on routes and procedures, and others, motivated by the mindless eroticism which is programmed into the genetic structure of the Latin male, frankly out for what they could get.

In the Via Positano she was pinched three times; in the Via delle 4 Fontane, twice; in the Via Nazionale (a long one), eleven; in the Corso Vittorio Emanuele, seven. Total, twenty-three.

Miss Thirkell was, of course, the last person to take indiscriminate pinching in her stride. Each pinch was a rape in little, a siege-gun aimed at the citadel of her chastity.

Each time it happened she jumped and turned round to identify her assailant, her confusion grew, her cheeks burned more hotly, her lips quivered a little faster. But she neither screamed, nor fled, nor gave way to hysteria. She bit her lip, blinked back her tears, took a firmer grip on the handles of the chair and pushed doggedly on.

She had a Mission to perform.

And gradually, as her embarrassment increased, so there grew in her, proportionately, a fighting spirit that she did not know she possessed. Fanned by adversity the spark of determination grew into a fiercely burning resolve. She would show these beastly foreigners how a lady behaves under provocation. Or die!

Icy Contempt, Serene Indifference, that was the order of the day.

So, surrounded by her private maelstrom, she plunged on through the teeming streets heading for the river.

When finally she came to the end of the Via della Conciliazione and saw the great square spread out before her and realised that she had arrived, that she had reached the last station on her personal Via Dolorosa, she was still in control of herself, but only just. Breakdown was no more than a knife-edge away.

There had even been moments in the last half hour when she had wished that Mr Heavenspur would wake up.

She took a deep breath and looked about her.

The next step was to find an informant with a view to locating the Via Adolfo Muni. The crowd stood round, grinning and gesticulating. No point in asking any of these ill-bred lunatics. Why must they *jabber* so? A policeman, that was it. A *nice* policeman. Friendly but not familiar. A rock to cling to.

She stood on tiptoe, trying to see over the heads of the people who pressed round her. She was perspiring freely. Several locks of hair had escaped from the bun which should have contained them and with one hand she kept nervously pushing them back from her forehead. A white bus drew up at the kerb and a few feet away. Its front door came open with a hiss and two nuns in brown habits got out carrying a wheelchair between them.

At that moment Miss Thirkell felt a pinch on her bottom.

Her control snapped. With a shrill yell of long-suppressed rage and humiliation she whirled for a nose-to-nose confrontation with her attacker. It was a policeman, as it happened; a little man, potbellied, his face almost entirely obscured by his moustache, his sunglasses and six inches of leering teeth; still rubbing between thumb and forefinger the memory of Miss Thirkell's right buttock. Red-handed.

Without any further preamble than the shrill cry noted above Miss Thirkell set to work to kill him. For a few moments it looked as though she might be the first woman to succeed in beating the life out of a Roman policeman by means of an Alitalia shoulder bag containing a toothbrush and a nylon nightie. But the policeman was a shade too quick for her. Rightly interpreting the flashing of Miss Thirkell's eyes as intent to commit GBH and worse, he rolled with the punch. In less than half a trice he had executed a nimble leap something between a belly-roll and an entrechat which took him temporarily out of range. At the same time he grabbed one of the handles of Cranley's chair and spun it between himself and Miss Thirkell's attack. She riposted by a mighty wrench on the other handle. The chair made a lightning turn through 720 degrees and, impelled by its centrifugal momentum, shot off at an angle and was swallowed up in the crowd, which parted to let it through.

Out of a corner of her mind Miss Thirkell saw it go. But the chair was no longer a Sacred Trust but merely an impediment to her lust for revenge. An impediment which was now removed.

Whirling her bag, she advanced again to the attack.

# 18

The venue chosen for the Special Audience is the Basilica of the Blessed Immolation, a small church within the walls of the Vatican City. The seats have been cleared from the nave. Swiss Guards line the walls. A throne has been placed on the chancel steps and, in it, H.H. On his left stand Cardinal Nuvoletto, conscious for once; on his right, Polenta.

A team of perspiring beadles under the Maestro di Camera is putting the last touches to the marshalling of the congregation. But among the latter group the fervour which has been mounting steadily in expectation of the event has reached such a pitch that the marshals find they have their work cut out to establish the necessary degree of calm, reverence and order.

H.H. surveys the preparations with his customary benevolence. A half-smile of loving condescension plays about his lips as he considers the hundred-odd specimens of suffering humanity before him. Not one among them but is maimed, or halt, or both —and that to a quite exceptional degree. They are, indeed, the *most* maimed and *most* halt that can be found. Some are the victims of genetic deformity, others of the disasters of war, others of civil misfortunes and acts of God—industrial accidents, earthquakes, vendetta-mutilations. Between them they muster a quite exceptional variety of prosthetic hardware— surgical boots, glass eyes, metal noses, false limbs of all kinds from the traditional peg-leg to sophisticated battery-operated models, forests of crutches fashioned in wood or metal, hand-driven skateboards for the legless, and wheelchairs by the score.

A little more than half of them are women.

H.H. waits patiently in silence for the congregation to settle down. Polenta scowls at his boots. Nuvoletto stares vaguely into the middle distance.

The beadles, meanwhile, darting about the edges of the flock like so many sheepdogs, have penned the cripples into a compact group at the foot of the steps. But the subdued disorder which has so far prevailed, instead of undergoing the hoped-for diminution, exhibits a marked and steady increase. Superadded to the mood of religious hysteria, until now partially suppressed, is the mutinous dissatisfaction of those who find themselves furthest from the action. Inequities of this kind, aggravated in some cases by a difference in height of anything up to three feet, produce determined attempts by certain individuals to modify the situation by making their way to the front. By hook, or by crook, as the case may be. But they are so tightly packed that movement is even more than usually difficult, and while the majority of those in the best places are unwilling to yield their advantage, those few who are willing to make way find themselves quite unable to do so.

Swaying breaks out. It is contagious, and spreads.

Soon the whole mass is being shaken this way and that by conflicting currents of kinetic energy straining at the leash. The beadles push harder at the edges, thinking to restore the equilibrium of the mass by the application of countervailing force, but only succeed in making matters worse. Oscillation, under pressure from its own feedback, becomes acute. The congregation is on the point of degenerating into a mob.

H.H. has observed that things are not quite as they should be. He exchanges his benevolent smile for a look of mild alarm mixed with puzzlement. He whispers something to Nuvoletto. Nuvoletto responds with an amiable nod. H.H. frowns and turns to Polenta. But Polenta is busy with some whispering of his own. An emissary in deacon's robes has sidled up behind him and is trying to draw Polenta's attention to someone or something in the crowd. This something is the figure of Cranley Heavenspur, enthroned in his wheelchair, plaster leg sticking out at a jaunty angle, head lolling, mouth open, eyes closed, a serene expression fixed upon his face. A picture of untroubled repose. Placed squarely in the centre of the group Cranley occupies, so to speak, the eye of the storm and stands out as an island of calm in the troubled waters which swirl about him on all sides. Miss Thirkell is nowhere to be seen.

Polenta gestures towards Cranley and then to the main door. He mutters some instructions and the aide hurries out by a side entrance.

H.H. decides that the Time Has Come. He gets to his feet, intending no doubt to initiate some move which will restore the situation. But the initiative is no longer his. In fact, never was. Instability has taken charge.

Even as he clears his throat and raises his hands in the beginnings of a Pontificial gesture, the situation takes a decisive, and by this time inevitable, turn for the worse.

Respect for the Time and Place has until now imposed a reverent silence on the crowd—if we ignore, that is, an unavoidable background orchestration of heavy breathing, foot-shuffling, joint-clicking and the squeak of ungreased axles. But suddenly this silence is permanently and irrevocably shattered by a high-pitched yell and the thud of a falling body. A lady hunchback in the front row, her timber leg hooked from under her by the insidious crutch of an unscrupulous neighbour, pitches forward on her face.

It is the signal for Instant Pandemonium.

Dropping all vestige of self-restraint the overstimulated mutilees abandon themselves to all-out warfare. No holds are barred, no infirmity is sacrosanct, no weapon is left unemployed. Crutches become clubs. Wheelchairs are immobilised or overturned by wooden legs thrust between their spokes. A woman with a metal arm unscrews it to batter a neighbour who defends herself with the crutch wrestled from another opponent who in turn loses her balance and topples to the floor. A legless dwarf sinks his teeth in an adversary's calf, leaves them there and scuttles off in search of other opponents. A horrifying chorus of groans, yells and curses rises to the vaulted ceiling, mingled with the crash of colliding wheelchairs, the splintering of crutches and the thud of falling bodies.

H.H. stands horror-struck on the chancel steps. His mouth opens and shuts in totally inaudible appeal for peace on earth, goodwill towards men.

Nuvoletto, evidently under the impression that some form of organised entertainment is in progress, looks on with the same benign but unfocused expression he has worn from the start.

Polenta, on the other hand, is leaping about on the steps in a frenzy of rage and indecision. His attention is painfully divided by an attempt to keep one eye on the entrance behind him, through which he expects reinforcements to appear, and the other on Cranley. This is no easy task, for the unresisting Cranley is being swept rapidly to and fro at the mercy of the inconstant tides of battle. At one point Polenta descends the steps as if to throw himself into the mêlée. At the last moment he thinks better of it and withdraws.

By now the Swiss Guards have thrown their weight into the struggle behind the beadles and it seems likely that, other things being equal, the forces of order will, eventually get the upper hand. But other things seldom are equal.

Suddenly, to Polenta's horror, Cranley's plaster leg takes the full force of a swingeing blow from an aluminium crutch and breaks open like a walnut. There is an explosive report, audible even above the din of battle, and the relic, itself unbroken and neatly wrapped in its plastic bag marked SPEEDY CLEANERS, tumbles to the ground.

At this, with a last desperate look over his shoulder, Polenta plunges into the fray like a cormorant into a shoal of piranha fish.

But the removal of the plaster shield has unleashed the full force of the mysterious box's uncanny power. Immersed in the heaving, screaming mass are fifty women. Until that moment they have been engaged in what was no more than a mindless, though bitter, struggle for survival. But now the dreaded Emanations are at work on them. With the shattering of Cranley's leg their very being is transformed by a sledgehammer stimulus to the elemental depths of their animal natures. They are seized by an orgiastic surge of destructive power, tossed like matchwood on invisible waves of ecstasy. The response is unanimous. Ignoring all other business, driven by a single over-riding compulsion, they begin with one accord to fight, kick, bite, scratch, tear and claw their way from wherever they happen to be towards the source of the energy that has engulfed them.

But Polenta is there before them. A tragic mistake, and his last.

He covers the few remaining feet that separate him from the relic in a flying leap and lands on top of it like a rugby forward on a loose ball. But the fall has winded him and the moment he takes to recover is fatal. Before he can rise, the first of the Maenads is on him, screaming, tearing, then another, a third, a fourth. . . . In a matter of seconds Cardinal Polenta has disappeared completely under the writhing pile.

Disappeared completely, and permanently. He was never seen again. Pieces were found, but nothing larger than a fair-sized meatball.

Later that day the Rome police detained a man found wandering about screaming in St Peter's Square. He was unable to give his name but was identified from his passport as Frederick Porson, an English Journalist.

# 19

'You know what this is?' asked Colonel Wou.

'It's a shovel, sir,' answered Chang.

'Excellent,' said Colonel Wou. 'How true. A shovel. And have you any experience in this kind of work?'

'Digging?' asked Chang. 'No, sir.'

'It's not *mere* digging, if you understand me. It is, rather, what I would call *specialised* digging.'

'Specialised,' said Chang.

'Latrines,' said Colonel Wou. 'To be exact.'

'Oh,' said Chang.

'Well?'

'Sir?'

'Have you any experience of that sort, Chang?'

'No, sir.'

The Colonel beamed at Chang paternally.

'It is no matter,' he said. 'We shall make a specialist of you yet. There is plenty of time.'

# 20

It was a grey morning, windy and cold. Rain swept in gusts across the tiny airfield and flattened itself in moving swathes against the long grass.

A grey-painted two-seater plane taxied across the turf to the end of the runway and waited, roaring its engines spasmodically. A knot of people emerged from a quonset hut at the edge of the field and made their way over the wet grass, hands on their hats, heads bent against the driving rain.

When they reached the waiting aircraft Flake turned to say his goodbyes. He had no luggage except a metal box about-eighteen inches long and eight inches square hugged into the folds of his raincoat. He began to shake the hands that were extended to him. Cranley's was the last in line.

'It's all yours, then, Heavenspur,' he shouted.

'Yes,' shouted Oxford's new Professor of Statistical Historiography. And he added: 'Thank you.'

'I can't hear.'

Cranley shrugged, smiled and shook his head.

'Well, goodbye,' shouted Flake.

He climbed awkwardly into the plane and waved once from

the door before it closed behind him.

'Goodbye,' they shouted. 'Goodbye.'

The plane roared, shook itself and trundled away from them across the bumpy turf.

In the cabin Flake smiled to himself, eyeing the parachute on the seat beside him: another miracle for Rasselas.

The plane had begun its take-off run when Porson, wearing a white raincoat, burst from the hedge at the furthest end of the field. From the cabin window Flake caught a glimpse of a dishevelled figure sprinting crazily across the grass towards him, waving its arms. Then the figure shrank suddenly and dropped away as the plane leapt forward, lingered a last moment and threw itself upwards into the grey sky.

Flake was still smiling. It was like going home.

# Appendix I

As an instance of the extent to which Professor Flake's mind was elsewhere during his ill-fated flight, we may cite the following miracle of mental arithmetic, formulated in mid-air somewhere in the region of Debra Markos:

$$\left| \frac{\delta^2 \overrightarrow{B}}{\delta \tau^2} \right| \equiv \sqrt{-1} \; \sum_{\varkappa=0}^{\varkappa=\infty} \log T \iiint \nabla \phi \; dy \; dx \; dz$$

(Where T represents a random constant of uncertain value.)

This proposition was, in later years, to cause a profound schism in the mathematical world, where it became known as Flake's Paradox (for the reason, some asserted, that it made no sense). The pro-Flake faction hailed it as a stunningly original approach to the problem of buoyancy viewed as a function of the mass-weight ratio of the vehicle in relation to the specific viscosity of the surrounding medium (in this case, air). The word breakthrough was freely employed.

The opposing party maintained with equal nerve that the whole thing was vitiated by Flake's failure to allow for the influence of the earth's gravitational field on an air-borne vehicle (in this case, a balloon). But to the pro-Flakers this objection bespoke an intellectual poverty which rendered it unworthy of serious refutation.

Flake himself believed, and went to his grave believing, that his formula was a triumphant vindication of the continuing utility of sophisticated liveware. Be this as it may, as an aid to aerial navigation, Flake's Paradox was a non-starter and its influence on the time and place of the balloon's descent, nil.

# Appendix II

S.I.D. (Servizio Informazioni Difesa)—Italian Military Intelligence. Formerly S.I.F.A.R. (Servizio Informazioni Forze Armate Riunite) but renamed at the time of the de Lorenzo scandal (1968). De Lorenzo, responsible for S.I.F.A.R., was found to have been so injudicious as to embroil his department in the maelstrom of Italian party politics. He had, for example, amassed dossiers on a large number of people who by no stretch of the imagination could be supposed security risks.

S.I.O.S. (Servizio Informazioni Osservazioni Sicurezza)—Italian intelligence agency charged with internal security.

JOINT—The Joint Distribution Committee. A Jewish relief organisation based on the U.S. Repeatedly accused of serving as a cover for intelligence operations, particularly in Eastern Europe; this accusation flatly rebutted by JOINT spokesmen. But suspicions that JOINT may have other concerns than the issue of knitted comforters to the victims of anti-Zionist discrimination were lent some colour when JOINT's vice-chairman, a Mr Jordan, was found floating face down in the Vitava river in Prague in August 1967. A Swiss pathologist named Hardmeier who later performed an autopsy on Mr Jordan was himself found dead in the countryside outside Zurich a few days after. JOINT's chairman, Mr Louis Brodio, accused the Czech government of 'covering up a vile crime'.

B.N.D., M.A.D. (Bundes Nachrichten Dienst, Militärischer Abschirm Dienst)—together with the Verfassungschutz (dedicated to Protection of the Constitution) are the principal West German intelligence agencies. The B.N.D., formerly known as the Germano-American Agency, was run by the 'Faceless General' Reinhardt Gehlen. Gehlen's favoured position (the B.N.D.'s slice of the federal budget was one hundred million marks in 1967) was based on the special knowledge of Communist military organisation which he built up during his service in O.K.H. Intelligence during the war. This knowledge, on the cessation of hostilities, proved exceedingly saleable. The Communists, too, valued Gehlen highly. In 1953 Wollweber, the East Berlin security chief, put a price of one million DM on his head. In May 1968 Gehlen was succeeded by another wartime specialist in Soviet affairs, General Gerhard Wessel, founder of the M.A.D.

LA MANO (La Mano Blanco)—one of a number of right-wing terrorist organisations currently active in Guatemala. Founded June 3, 1966. Victims are normally tortured to death. This is known as 'suicide'. La Mano's exploits include the assassination of a local beauty queen, Rogelia Cruz (formerly Miss Guatemala); an abortive plot to dynamite a number of churches; and the kidnapping of the Archbishop of Guatemala, Mgr. Mario Casariego (March 16th, 1968). The prelate was recovered but La Mano's leader Raul Lorenzana met his end when a police car, in which he was being taken into captivity to answer for the kidnapping, was machine-gunned by unknown assailants. La Mano subsequently accused the Archbishop of having been 'intellectually responsible' for their leader's demise. Other prominent members of this organisation are Roberto Alejos, Knight of the Equestrian Order of St Sylvester (a Vatican order), and Carlos Cifuentes, Secretary of Information in the government of Carlos Castillo Armas. (Armas was installed in power in June 1954 by the joint efforts of the C.I.A. and the United Fruit Company. He proved insufficiently conservative for some tastes and in 1957 was found murdered in his office in the Presidential Palace.)

P.I.D.E.—Portugese political police. The useful services of this worthy body include political assassinations, such as that of the opposition leader General Delgado, and the running of a much-frequented concentration camp at Tarrafal.

H.O.P., H.R.B.—Croatian underground 'liberation' movements. A member of the latter, Nedeljko Mrkonjik, was recently found full of bullet holes in a wood outside Paris. This event, coming shortly after a bomb outrage which wrecked a toilet in the Yugoslav Club in Paris, has been tentatively attributed to rivalry between the two fraternities. In 1967 a similar misfortune overtook the West German head of the H.R.B. in Stuttgart.

H.I.A.G.—Old-comrades association of the German S.S. Those desiring more information may subscribe to the H.I.A.G. newspaper 'Der Freiwillige' (The Volunteer). A separate, but affiliated, organisation exists for the benefit of ex-Totenkopf members (German wartime equivalents of Butlin's Redcoats).

SPINNE (Spider) and ODESSA—networks set up at the end of the war to satisfy the urge for foreign travel that agitated the ranks of the Nazi notables. Herr Adolf von Thadden, who may be assumed to know as much as anyone on this subject, is on record as declaring that Spinne and Odessa never existed outside the imaginations of sensation-seeking journalists. This news will surprise some persons of German origin currently residing in Latin America and the Middle East. No significance can be attached to the fact that Von Thadden was in Cairo in 1947 at the same time as Johannes von Leers, formerly assistant to Dr Goebbels and one of the principal architects of both the mythical Spinne and the mythical Odessa. Nor to Herr von Thadden's relations with the enigmatic Dr Fakusa, diplomatic representative of the Arab League in Bonn and head of the Egyptian secret service. It cannot, therefore, have been von Thadden who introduced Dr Fakusa to neo-Nazi circles in Germany and enabled him to arrange for the export to Egypt of a number of technicians specialising in ballistic missiles.